# THE SECOND BOOK OF THE

# ALIENBUTT SAGA

## Glenn Scrimshaw

# THE RISE OF MR FLUFFY

GINGERNUT BOOKS Ltd
www.gingernutbooks.co.uk

# INTRODUCTION.

A long time ago in a galaxy about two months away at light speed....

Dribede Dagnabbit was an Ick who had dreams, real big dreams. He was living in a time of great change within the Ick Empire with the first colonisation of a new planet just being given the go ahead by the Emperor. People were saying an Ick of quick wits and possessing good luck could go far in this new world. His people were starting to reach out into space and those who led the way would become heroes. Dribede embraced this new dawn with excitement, and aimed to rise above his mundane station. All his life he had been known as the thick brother of the local fruit farmer, but this was his chance to become a famous hero. Dribede had spent his entire life in his elder brother's shadow, but not for much longer. He would show everyone he was the one with a future. Dreams did sometimes come true, yet not always in the way that people wanted them to. His brother had got the brains in the family and by suddenly dropping dead earlier that evening, some would say he got the luck too.

Dribede lay in his bed. He had woken with a start and now wondered how three very strange figures had just walked through a solid wall and into his room. The first one was dressed in strange furs and wearing an even stranger helmet with horns attached to each side, and he sounded upset.

"It wasn't my fault, he just panicked when he saw you and

ran onto my sword. There was nothing that I could do to stop him."

The second figure, who wore something like a monk's habit, waved his hand dismissively. "Trobjorn, you never take responsibility for your actions. It's just a good job he has a brother who can stand in for him or you would be in big trouble."

All three then stopped talking and stared at Dribede, who lay on the bed looking confused. It was then that the third figure spoke, a woman of strange looks. She wore a bright colourful dress that seemed to float and swirl around even though there was no wind to make it move. She stared at Dribede, who hadn't moved since they entered the room, and didn't even try to hide the look of disappointment at what she saw before her.

"He doesn't look much like a prophet that's going to foretell the destruction of his people to me, brother. Who would ever take him seriously?"

"Give him a wonky eye and some warts," put in Trobjorn helpfully, "and make him dribble and eat his shoe. That's how a good prophet should always behave. People then know they're real and not faking it to get the table scraps before the hounds."

"Excuse me," put in Dribede nervously. "Why are you talking about destroying my people? And how did you walk through that wall to get in here?"

All three stopped talking and looked at him, then at each other, before the one who looked like a monk spoke. "He can see us. Fate, I thought you were making us invisible after what happened earlier?"

"I thought you were doing the invisible trick. It was your idea to hide us this time so Trobjorn doesn't kill anyone else important," Fate replied, not willing to take the blame for forgetting to make them invisible.

"Not fair. I said it wasn't my fault and even apologised," Trobjorn replied sulkily.

"We don't need to worry about it anyway. You're going to scramble his brain in a minute so he won't remember us, and you took Trobjorn's sword off him," replied the woman dismissively.

The one in the helmet named Trobjorn nodded in agreement. "Good point Fate, he doesn't look like an excitable jumping around bloke like his brother. Bit of a poor excuse for an Ick really. You'll be doing him a favour once you send him doolally with our prophecy."

"I can hear you all too, you know," said Dribede nervously, finally moving to sit up.

"Don't worry, nothing is going to happen for a good few thousand years yet," the monk said, giving a friendly smile. "You'll be long dead by then so it won't make any difference to how long you live. And as for any children, well, let's face it, that was never going to happen, was it?"

"It's an epic tale, son," Trobjorn cut in, quickly changing the subject as Dribede looked crestfallen at Destiny's opinion of him ever finding a girlfriend. "Full of treachery and betrayal, ending in the last stand of the righteous Odin."

"It's not Odin, his name is Wickede," corrected the woman. This interruption got an angry glance from Trobjorn before he continued.

"And the mighty warrior Thor."

"It's Blackarachnia not Thor," the woman corrected again. "Look, let's just drop off the prophecy and get back to our drinks before one of his mob pinch 'em." She continued pointing at Trobjorn who nodded, knowing that stealing drinks was the least of things his men did. The monk agreed and stepped forward and placed his hand on Dribede's head.

The unfortunate Ick's body went stiff before slumping back onto the bed drooling and cross-eyed.

"Right, let's go and get rat-arsed then," the monk said happily with a grin at his two companions.

As the three figures turned and walked away back through the wall Trobjorn's voice carried back into the room.

"You forgot to add the warts, and I still think you should let me fight in the final battle, accompanied by a host of Valkyries in skimpy armour."

"No," the monk answered. "That isn't your destiny, but the skimpily armoured shield maidens sound usable."

"But you could change it so it was my destiny. Come on, I know you make people's destiny up as you go along. Let's face it, Destiny is your middle name," he pressed hopefully.

"No it isn't, it's my only name," Destiny replied.

"I have another job for you. I want you to drop off a message for me," a new fourth voice cut in.

"Dream, what the hell are you doing here!" Destiny asked angrily.

"Where else would I be? That mortal is going to dream the future, which means I need to send him the dreams. Now, as that's all finished with, can I join you for drinks?"

"It's your round then, and you can't use Trobjorn as a messenger, it's not his destiny. You can go find your own mortal to hang out with. Trobjorn is busy," Destiny sullenly said, not wanting to share his new friend with his brother.

"I can if Trobjorn has a dream tonight where he meets someone in the future to give them a message," thought Dream with a sly smile.

Dribede became the most famous Ick in their long illustrious history, although he was also the most unpopular Ick ever. His message wasn't a welcome one and the phrase don't shoot the messenger didn't exist to the Ick or Dribede's prophecy would have been much shorter, as they would not have been able to stop themselves. As it was, Dribede lived a long life before choking to death on his shoes thirty years after delivering his first prophetic rant. The book about his dreams became a guide to his people, but one where the dreams continued to evolve even after his death, as the chaos of a Nexus who would change the future was set down, and the hope of avoiding defeat was instilled within the Ick people. They knew at the end of days the Nexus would stagger drunkenly across the universe, aided by the chosen few heroes, thwarting those who would try to destroy them.

# Chapter 1

## The Return of the Hunter.

### INTERSTELLAR NEWS CHANNEL 9.
### NEWS FLASH.

News has come in that the dead Ick leader, Wickede, personally led the latest Ick counter-attack. In fierce fighting the Federation forces have made strategic withdrawals as they prepare for their next offensive. In a short statement to the Senate the gains made by the Ick were dismissed as part of the Federation Navies' long-term plans, and an end to the war of the coffee bean was in sight.

In related news the High Priest of the Order of Righteous Indignation has condemned the use of necromancy by the Ick and declared that all who stand with the Ick are heretics in the eyes of the Celestial Jellyfish of Judgement. When a local frozen seafood merchant mentioned that maybe the Ick leader was not killed when reported assassinated, he was battered to death by an angry mob led by the High Priest, who was allegedly wielding a frozen jellyfish. The death of the merchant is being reported as the Celestial Jellyfish's judgement on unbelievers by church officials. Wide-scale panic buying of tinned foods in preparation for a zombie apocalypse caused by Wickede's resurrection has been played down by authorities as ridiculous.

General Jee read the reports with growing anger. The Ick had counter–attacked, driving back the Federation forces. Smashing victories had the entire Federation forces in a full retreat all along the Ashia Minor front. The return of Wickede had galvanised their forces and with the cure for coffee addiction readily available on the Outer System Universal Wide Network, entire divisions of the Federation's conscripted army had defected to the Ick cause. Only his swift action in shutting down the Federal Wide Web in the Inner Systems until appropriate viruses could be uploaded to wipe such information, had prevented the news spreading to the heart of the Federation. Now only controlled sites still operated as the Federation spread stories of a wide-scale cyber-attack by the Ick. The Secret Order of the Bean would weather the storm in the Inner System but needed time to reposition its forces. They already controlled the Senate and kept those troops most loyal in all key positions. The robotic forces would now be recalled and production of them increased. He wasn't worried about losing the war; they still had the upper hand and the Ick did not have the forces to press their advantage. What infuriated him was the fact that he would have to postpone his own plans to seize control of the Order of the Bean and control the universe as its first emperor. The only positive thing so far was that there was no mention of the Alienbutt in any report, but he was still waiting for his spies to find out what that meant. Too angry to deal with the work before him, he stood up and decided to go release some of his pent-up anger.

Jee walked down to the detention area. Here on his private estates on the planet AV32 he was guaranteed total privacy, as the estate sprawled over an entire continent. The planet was owned by the Secret Order and the estates were a perk of his position. He exited the lift and entered the giant underground holding area. It was empty and bare apart from a large circular holding cell in the centre, which contained one prisoner. After a month of regular beatings and the expert attention of his torturer his sister still showed no signs of breaking. With a broad grin Jee walked over to the energy shield that was the barrier of the cell.

"Great news sister, it appears that Wickede stabbed that Alienbutt in the back to return, and left him for dead. Maybe the Ick leader is not so unlike me." Jee had no proof of this but suspected something fatal had happened to Alienbutt. He had sent Alienbutt's father, upgraded by cyborg implants and reprogrammed to be a killing machine, to track down Alienbutt and Wickede and kill them. The fact that Wickede had made it back while Alienbutt was missing, made him suspect that Bigrip Alienbutt had managed to find them and at least carry out half of his mission. Without Alienbutt the Ick were doomed and he hoped his little comment would get an angry reaction from his sister.

Grommit sat on the floor with her legs crossed as she stared at her brother, the same look on her face that she had every time he came to see her. That look of pure murder was still there aimed at him, undiminished by her time here. He knew if she got the chance she would try to kill him in an instant.

"Still not talking? Well, should we cut straight to your daily beating then?" he asked, averting his eyes from the murderous gaze. With a grin Jee pulled a pair of gauntlets from his belt, pulling them on. The metal plating over the knuckles and fingers began to spark with an electric current. As the shields were dropped between himself and his sister three other figures stepped forward each holding electro-batons ready for when Grommit would launch herself at her brother.

Hydroponic's ship had finally managed to reach the giant space station of the bounty hunters. The stasis booth containing

Nifty had been transferred to the medical lab and Hydroponic stood back with Duke Ramboe and Blackarachnia as the doctors examined the data from the booth. On the journey Hydroponic had repeatedly tried to draw Blackarachnia out of the black mood that he had descended into. Both had been around death enough to know Nifty's chances were slim using regular medical science. Hydroponic had tried to explain the use of his powder Mfkzt but he knew that his old partner was not listening. Now they stood in the medical facility watching the doctor and dreading what he would say. Finally the doctor finished his examination and walked over to where they waited.

"I'm afraid the injuries are extensive. If we turn off the stasis field to treat her she has maybe a ten per cent chance of survival."

Hydroponic and Duke Ramboe looked at Blackarachnia. The bounty hunter didn't move or react at first but finally he looked over at Duke Ramboe.

"I want a ship; do you give me one or do I take one?" he said quietly. He knew without doubt though that he would be leaving with a ship.

"Blackarachnia, wait, let me try my way," pleaded Hydroponic. He placed a restraining hand onto his arm. Blackarachnia turned to stare at Hydroponic, and in spite of himself Hydroponic took a step back at what he saw in that glare.

"Do what you will with your powder. I'm not waiting here to watch her die," he stated. Returning his gaze to Duke Ramboe, he continued. "Now do you give me a ship?"

"You know where mine is, it's the best ship here at the station. Will you be requiring a crew?" Duke Ramboe asked, knowing that to argue with Blackarachnia just now would be suicide. Blackarachnia didn't answer the question, as he was already walking out of the door. After he had left Duke

Ramboe sighed in relief and looked at Hydroponic.

"What the hell has happened? He's always been one that I would sooner step around than face, but..." he trailed off to silence.

"He wouldn't talk about what happened on our way over here, but he was clinging to his sanity as he hoped that we could heal Nifty. Then we heard that someone called Alienbutt was also lost or missing." Hydroponic shrugged his shoulders before continuing. "Losing both has sent him over the edge. He's insane with grief and dealing with it the only way he knows how. Blackarachnia the Hunter is now out to kill anyone he feels responsible for all this and will go through anything and anyone to get them."

"He was always a cold one, you knew him better than most. But he had started to change since he teamed up with Alienbutt and met Nifty; he had started to become more human. He even seemed to have discovered some emotions for the first time," Duke Ramboe added sadly. "I guess he's never had to deal with guilt and the grief of losing someone before." Both stood staring at the doorway where Blackarachnia had left. Finally Hydroponic turned to the Doctor and passed a small vid-screen over to him.

"If you want to save the girl, set this up to these exact instructions and then call me when it's ready."

The Doctor looked over to Duke Ramboe, who nodded his approval. He began looking at the screen reading the instructions while Duke Ramboe walked over to the stasis booth. He placed a hand on the lid and stared at the face of Nifty; she looked like she was just asleep, not seconds from death.

"What are you up to, Hydroponic? You left here years ago almost as broken as Blackarachnia is now, yet now you return and hint that you can raise the dead," Duke Ramboe asked, not looking away from Nifty.

"I'm gonna save the girl's life. Now I need some proper food, and you can tell me what's happening in the universe to turn it even crazier than it was, and I may tell you what I did on my holiday."

Blackarachnia soon reached Duke Ramboe's ship. He was unaware of events going on around him as he marched through the station, and wouldn't remember how everyone quickly moved out of his way as he approached. Those onboard the stations were all bounty hunters, each at the top of their game. They had all spent years hunting down the most dangerous criminals in the universe and now fought a brutal war, but all sensed that here was the apex hunter of their kind. Here was the ultimate hunter in the universe, his ferocity unmasked for all to see. All that saw the look on his face knew they didn't want to become the focus of his attention, even for a moment. As he reached Duke Ramboe's ship he saw ground crews already preparing it for flight and loading supplies onto it. The ship was a custom model, built to its owner's own design, at sixty feet it looked sleek and fast, and Blackarachnia knew it packed enough firepower to give even a dreadnought pause. It usually had a crew of just four personnel but could be fully automatic and just flown by one person. A nervous member of the ground crew approached Blackarachnia and gave a trembling salute.

"Sir, Ramboe called ahead to say that you would be using his ship. It will be ready for flight within the hour." He stood waiting for a response, becoming more nervous as the silence continued.

"I will wait on board," Blackarachnia finally said and walked onto the ship without another word.

Since escaping with the injured Nifty, Blackarachnia had

swung between the terror of losing his new wife and anger for allowing this to happen; then guilt had kicked in at the fact he hadn't killed the assassin when he had the chance. He had been aware of his old companion Hydroponic trying to coax things out of him but it was all a haze. Then as they approached the space station he had heard of Wickede's return and the news that Alienbutt was not with him. There were no details in the report he had seen, just that Wickede was back but Alienbutt wasn't.

He had spent his entire life alone, making no friends, caring for nothing. He became a bounty hunter because it was easy for him and he quickly became the best. He tested himself against the most dangerous criminals, hoping that he would finally feel something, that it would fill the void within him. Then by chance he had run into Nifty at some stupid function where he was acting as a bodyguard to Wickede and the sight of her blew him away. In an instant he changed as he finally felt something, that he later discovered was a little something called love. He couldn't get her out of his head, but she wanted nothing to do with him. Then soon after meeting her, he had come across Alienbutt and something else clicked in his head. Before he knew it Alienbutt had become his friend as he had taught the strange alien what he would need to survive in the coming war. The ice-cold bounty hunter and drunken ex-taxi driver had made the most unlikely of friendships as each influenced the other in their search to become complete people. He was a different person when next he met Nifty and this time she did give him the time of day, and the void inside him began to disappear. Now Alienbutt was gone and Nifty was alive only because of a stasis booth. The life he had glimpsed so briefly was gone, but he would make those responsible pay for taking it away from him and leaving this strange pain he could not switch off. He knew of the Secret

Order who were behind all these events. He had a name to start off with and that would be all he needed. He would start there with the unfortunate owner of that name and then hunt down everyone connected with the Order.

Hydroponic was called back to the medical lab two hours later. Blackarachnia had left the station and jumped to light speed immediately he was airborne. Hydroponic knew the only way to save his old partner was to save his wife. He knew Blackarachnia would hunt down those he saw as responsible without a care for his own life, just wanting to wash away his pain in blood and death. As he walked into the medical lab he saw a large clear immersion tank set up next to the stasis booth.

"Is it all set up to match the instructions I left you with?" he asked the Doctor. When he got a nod from the Doctor he walked over and took a small package from his belt pocket. Pouring the contents into the tank he asked for the power to the tank to be switched on. A stream of bubbles rose up from the bottom of it. He stood and watched as the tank's liquid contents began to churn and the white powder he had poured into it dissolved. Duke Ramboe walked in as Hydroponic watched the tank's contents, and came to stand beside him.

"What happens now, Hydro?" he asked Hydroponic.

Without a word Hydroponic pulled a knife from his belt and slashed the palm of his hand. The wound was deep, and as the blood began to drip onto the floor he dipped his hand into the bubbling liquid, which began to glow. After a few seconds he withdrew his hand and showed it to Duke Ramboe and the Doctor, revealing no sign of the cut or even a scar.

"Witness the healing power of Mfkzt," Hydroponic said as the two men stared in amazement at his hand. "We need to place the girl in the tank. Immersion in the liquid won't drown her, but I don't know how long it will take for her to heal."

"What is this powder and where can we get more?" asked the Doctor, amazed. "This could save thousands of lives."

"We heal the girl and then I will explain everything I know of it to you." He handed the empty package to the Doctor and stood back waiting for them to transfer Nifty to the tank.

As the stasis field was turned off and the lid opened on the booth Nifty gave a weak cough, leaving flecks of blood on her pale lips. Quickly she was transferred into the tank and the fluid within the tank began to glow and shimmer around her wounds. The Doctor stood watching a computer screen that showed her vital signs. After a minute he looked over to Hydroponic.

"Her vitals are beginning to stabilise, heart rate and blood pressure are low but not getting any worse." He watched the screen for a while longer. "Signs of tissue regeneration, heart rate stable, wait, no, it's getting stronger, increasing."

"There goes immortality," Hydroponic muttered and gave a deep sigh.

"What?" asked Duke Ramboe, not removing his gaze, fascinated by what he watched as the glow increased from the tank.

"Nothing, let's go get a drink, leave the Doctor to his work." With that he turned and walked out. With a last glance at the tank Duke Ramboe turned and followed him.

# CHAPTER 2

## A Moment for Whiskey.

### INTERSTELLAR NEWS CHANNEL 9.
### NEWS FLASH.

In light of yesterday's attack on the coffee bean facilities on the planet Sloppystool and the murder of all the prominent personnel there, the E.D.F. today announced there will be increased security at all facilities. It is believed that the one-time bounty hunter Blackarachnia was responsible for the attack and is now acting as an assassin for the Ick. It is believed the Ick are now co-ordinating terrorist attacks against the Coffee Houses and Federal forces in a bid to disrupt life in the inner systems. An earlier cyber-attack by Ick operatives has led to the collapse of the Federal Wide Web with engineers still struggling to restore service. Communication within the Inner Systems has been dealt a major blow with only military service unaffected.

Blackarachnia is also wanted for questioning in relation to the murder of his wife, known to millions on Earth as Nifty the Niffler, who was Earth's oldest surviving lady. Nifty shot to fame with the story of how she had been kidnapped from pre-space Earth in her youth and ended up frozen in suspended animation aboard a trading vessel that was lost in space for six centuries.

General Jee, head of inner system security has issued a kill on sight order, stating that Blackarachnia is dangerous and not to be approached without full backup.

Wickede sat at the head of the table sipping a glass of whiskey. He had returned to this dimension and immediately launched a counter-attack against the Federation, rolling back their forces with a series of victories. Sending out Frank's formula to cure the coffee addiction symptoms, a number of fleets conscripted to the Federation Navies had cleaned up their crews and switched sides, but on the whole these new forces were not very well trained or equipped. Now they had to train and equip these new forces to get them up to fighting standard, which would be a drain on their overstretched resources. The war had now come to a standstill as each side prepared for the next move, neither side able to deal the killing blow. The down side to this lull in hostilities was now Wickede had the time to worry about his missing friends.

Alienbutt was lost in another dimension and they didn't know if he had survived the battle with the cyborg Alienbutt. Still recovering from the effects of the cyborg fart attack, Wickede had needed three blood transfusions and even now, almost a month after his return, he found himself tiring easily. Without the Alienbutt gas essence there was no way to mount a rescue mission despite Frank's obsessive attempts to simulate the fuel enhancer. Frank now worked in a new laboratory, working alone apart from the robot Kirk, who insisted that Frank take regular breaks to watch Star Trek and now the old earth series Lost in Space. Irony seemed to be totally lost on the robot. Snoodgrass feared for the scientist's sanity with him being closeted away with just the robot, while Wickede knew better. Frank's sanity had never been fully there to begin with so it wouldn't be a problem if he lost a little more of it.

Blackarachnia had disappeared off the radar, full of grief when he thought his wife was dead. The only good news was that thanks to his old partner Hydroponic's swift action, Nifty not only still lived, but her injuries were healed. She was still in a coma showing no signs of waking, but the doctors insisted she was out of danger and would make a full recovery. While no one knew where Blackarachnia was, it was not taking long before they discovered where he had been, as he was not being subtle in his actions and retribution. Snoodgrass was receiving regular reports from his spies on the bounty hunter's actions. Now members of the Coffee Houses were screaming out for extra security as word of the fate of their companions spread.

If the news that the Coffee House personnel were living in fear was a small speck of good news it was outweighed by the information that Grommit had been captured. A film of her being tortured had been leaked and had almost caused a mutiny, as the remnants of the Fo'c'sle prepared to mount a rescue mission, despite the fact that they had no idea of her whereabouts. Wickede had promised to support the rescue mission but only when they discovered where she was and Commander Kali came up with a viable plan. Her first plan of "We go in and kill everyone," had been sent back by Wickede, as he insisted on more detail. Kali had accepted that she needed to expand her plan and so sent in a revised one: "We go in and kill everyone, as painfully as we can." Wickede, knowing that he was not going to win, accepted the proposal with a grin, leaving Snoodgrass muttering about half-baked plans. Despite this outward show of despair at the lack of any real planning Snoodgrass was using every agent at his disposal to try and pinpoint Grommit's location. Kali had already assembled a team ready for a rescue attempt and was just awaiting news, and he knew he needed to get information about Grommit soon.

Wickede looked up as Snoodgrass walked in. His oldest friend and advisor had aged during the last couple of years. The responsibility of leading the Ick during Wickede's absence had told on him. His hair was now showing more grey than black and the lines around his eyes had got deeper. The eyes themselves though were still sharp and alert and he had lost none of his considerable intellect or ability to run the Ick intelligence service.

"Take a seat and give me some good news," Wickede said, indicating a chair next to him with the whiskey glass. Snoodgrass sat down with a slight smile and produced the little computer notepad that he always seemed to carry with him.

"It appears that someone has now started killing Senators. Four have been found executed over the last week, as well as a number of their senior staff. The assassin seems to have moved on from just killing staff employed by the Coffee houses and destroying coffee production facilities. It seems he has moved on to the next tier of the Coffee House hierarchy."

"Blackarachnia strikes again?" asked Wickede. He did not need the nod from Snoodgrass to know the answer.

"My sources in the Coffee Houses say he has the place in turmoil and there's some big roaches coming out of the woodwork. It looks like there's to be an emergency meeting of the Order behind the Coffee Houses. A number of prominent people we suspect to be members have suddenly cleared their appointments and are heading off to some secret location. Even Jee has reportedly cut short his holidays on his estates on AV32."

"Do we know where they are headed?" asked Wickede. If they could find out the location of the meeting and launch an attack, then they could make a major strike towards ending the war.

"I'm working on it, but I do know that it was Jee holding Grommit and there's a good chance she is still being held on his estates at AV23 where he was holidaying. I'm awaiting confirmation from an agent I have there. With Jee having left the planet to head for his meeting, there should only be a handful of guards left there to deal with."

"Have you informed Kali yet?"

"Her ship left about ten minutes ago, accompanied by all available Fo'c'sle personnel. She's meeting up with others before heading there once it's confirmed. I've forwarded all information we have on his estates to her ship, plus those holiday snaps we took five years ago when you were invited there as his guest. It's strange how fast things change in the world of politics."

Wickede smiled in spite of himself. "He was overly proud of his estates there. Let's hope they don't cause too much damage as they rip it apart looking for Grommit."

Snoodgrass returned the smile. "One last thing. The King of the Heeter system has approached us about them making a change of sides in the war. He would like us to send an emissary to negotiate. If we could get his shipyards working for us it would be a massive blow for the Coffee Houses and would give us a base within the inner systems."

"He's a lecherous old sod, but you're right, he's a major power. If he switches sides others may follow his lead. Do you have thoughts on who to send?" Wickede asked, refilling his glass.

"I seem to remember he took quite a shine to Kali. We could send that mad Fo'c'sle pilot in Killashandra's command with her too; he knows the local customs very well."

"Mention it to her when she gets back Let's just hope she doesn't kill the old king for groping her before he swaps sides."

"That's why I thought of Kali rather than Killashandra or any of the other female commanders we have," Snoodgrass continued, giving a smile. "She's far more level-headed and Ponnfarr is well known in Heeter, so with him as bodyguard she will be treated with the uttermost respect."

Wickede refilled his glass. "I thought we never looked into what our Fo'c'sle members did before they joined us?"

Snoodgrass shrugged. "We don't. They have a promise the Ick Empire will take them as seen, in return for their loyalty. The Empire would never break its word to them, so I employ outside agencies to enquire into their past and find out why they run to us."

"So what's Ponnfarr's story?" asked Wickede, intrigued.

"The most deadly arena warrior in Heeter history. Seems he upset the wrong person when he partied with the daughter of a powerful warlord and someone took pictures of their little escapade."

Wickede nodded. "So he upset the father?"

"No, the Queen's sister, she was trying to tempt Ponnfarr into her bedchamber. She took the news and his rejection of her rather badly and tried to poison the lover boy before an arena battle. When that didn't work she hired assassins who failed too, then she offered a bonus to any arena warrior that could kill him. They all failed, but Ponnfarr decided to leave before the Queen's sister launched thermal missiles at his estates."

Wickede looked shocked. "She wouldn't go that far, surely?"

"She did. He had left the planet only minutes before the strike. With the Queen's sister now dead it will be safe for him to return, and no one will bother Kali with Ponnfarr at her side. The people of Heeter are a strange lot, wrapped up in a rigid honour code. No one will cross Kali without facing Ponnfarr first and only another gladiator of the arena can challenge him." Snoodgrass smiled. "The old King will be happy to see his favourite nephew return home. My spies tell me he has an interesting plan for our mad little pilot and he is essential to them joining us."

# CHAPTER 3

## The City of the Frogs.

INTERSTELLAR NEWS CHANNEL 9. NEWS
FLASH.

The victorious Third and Sixth fleet of the Federation
Navies who were involved in the victorious battle of
Zaldarn and responsible for the destruction of the
second Ick Fleet under the command of the traitorous
commander Grommit today returned to Federation space
for much needed rest and refitting. Quezzel Proodich,
vice-leader of the Galactic Senate is taking the chance
to meet up with members of the fleet and give them the
thanks of the people of the Federation. Despite rationing
and restrictions in movement, support for our forces is
holding firm on all loyal planets within the Federation.

Billions of federation citizens are expected to tune in and
watch the special broadcast of the returning heroes that
is to be shown on all channels. Despite a counter-attack
by the Ick, many see the victory at Zaldarn as a decisive
moment in bringing the war to a victorious end.

Princess Isme walked into the room that had been set aside for the strange alien. They had brought him back to their home-world after bandaging his wounds so their healers could treat him. For weeks he had been close to death as he lay in a fever, but late the night before, the fever had broken and the healers were confident he would survive. Isme looked to the still-bandaged wrist where he had lost his hand and thought it strange that he did not seem to be showing any sign of growing a new one.

The Queen and Royal Court had been deeply troubled to hear of the attack on their guests and had ordered all of their people to leave the planet until they could find out if another attack would be coming. While the strangers had been guests with them they had learnt much about them and the strange worlds that they came from. It appeared that they lived lives where war and death seemed a common thing. Isme was fascinated by the stories they told, but many of her people were scared and worried at what their arrival might mean. Still, this Alienbutt had been a guest who was attacked on one of their worlds and he would be nursed back to health before it was decided what to do with him.

Isme hunched down next to the bed where Alienbutt lay sleeping. The air in the room was far too dry for her people and she felt her skin drying out. Without thought she began to use her tongue to lick around her mouth and then continued on to lick around the rest of her face, paying particular attention to her large eyes that stood out from the top of her frog-like face. Her people were a reptilian race with long powerful legs, a short body and long slender arms. Their skin colour was various shades of green and brown and they lived as much in water as on land. She finished wetting herself down and when she looked back to where Alienbutt lay, she saw he was watching her. Quickly she picked up a small purple fruit from a bowl beside the bed, quartered it and held a section up to his lips. After a moment Alienbutt began to suck at the juicy flesh.

"How do you feel?" she asked as he finished the fruit section. She offered him a second piece but he shook his head.

"Like someone gave me a right good kicking." His voice was weak. He then closed his eyes and she thought he would drift back off to sleep. "What happened?" he asked.

"I'll explain later when you're stronger, but you're safe now."

He nodded his head and again drifted off to sleep. Isme felt so much happier that he was recovering. Life had been so dull before the strangers arrived and now she had glimpsed their life through the stories she didn't want to lose her chance to see more of it.

Alienbutt quickly began to recover his strength. The frog people were polite to him but he could tell they were nervous having him around. Only the Princess Isme was friendly and as soon as he was able to get out of bed she began to show him around her home. Much of the city was underwater and those parts above the water were on islands within a string of great lakes and seas. The buildings above water were all organic in appearance and blended into the landscape. Nowhere did the frog people seek to build anything that would not fit naturally into their planet.

Alienbutt sat on the shore of one of the great lakes. He had been out of bed for almost a week and his strength had now almost returned. Suddenly Isme landed beside him, making him jump in shock at her sudden appearance. He doubted he would ever get used to the way her people could leap such large distances.

"A trader has arrived. He has contacts in many systems and may know someone who can help you return home," she said excitedly. "He's visited here lots of times and has offered to help you. Tonight he will sing for us and entertain us with his stories. It's always fun when he visits."

Alienbutt smiled but Isme could tell that the news didn't excite him that much.

"If anyone can get you home then he will know of them, Alienbutt. He may even know someone who can get your hand to grow back."

Alienbutt stared down at the still-bandaged stump. It was strange how his fingers still tingled, but he had heard that was normal for people who had lost body parts.

"Well, my Princess, let's go see this trader and not keep him waiting," he said, smiling at her, trying to sound positive.

The main hall where the frog people gathered to meet visitors from the outside worlds was a massive dome created from hundreds of giant green leaves, each easily thirty feet across. They allowed sunlight through them to give the inside a soft greenish light. As Alienbutt walked in he saw the envoy, standing in the centre of the dome. He was a tall human with long white hair and beard. He felt it strange that here in this dimension he was looking at someone who was definitely human. He was certain this was not some species that looked like them; he was looking at the real thing. As he approached, the figure turned to face him, breaking off conversation with four of the leaders of the frog people who stood around him. Alienbutt was taken aback by what he saw. He looked to be an older human by the white hair and long well-kept beard, but the eyes said so much more. Those eyes belonged to someone who had seen ages pass; this human, he knew, had seen hundreds of years of life. They both stood regarding each other for a while in silence.

"So you must be my friends' visitor, Alienbutt, isn't it?" the trader finally said with a smile. "My name is Stoney, I trade around these here systems."

"You've made your new home a long way from Earth, Stoney," Alienbutt said, returning the smile, and saw a flicker cross the old man's face.

"Well that's a name I haven't heard in many years. Have you come from there?" he asked in some surprise. Alienbutt nodded. Stoney hid his shock and then turned to the frog leaders. "I think I need to have a long sit down with your guest. It appears we have much in common."

Alienbutt had stood, and waited while the trader Stoney had completed some business, overseeing the delivery of a number of crates brought in from his ship. After the initial shock, Alienbutt's mind had begun to work overtime. If this trader was human, then there was a way for him to get home. Finally with his initial business complete, he made his excuses to the frog people and walked over to take a seat next to Alienbutt.

"Well, my strange new friend, it seems we have stories to share. Maybe we should tell our tales before you start to ask questions."

"I need to know how you got here. I have to get back," Alienbutt cut in, not wanting to wait and share stories. "A war rages and I must get back to help my friends."

"The way I came here will not be possible to use." Stoney held up his hands to put off Alienbutt's response. "Let me tell you my story and explain why you can't return that way." Alienbutt nodded and swallowed his impatience as Stoney began his story.

"I was the entertainments officer on a scientific research mission to an area of space known as Ashia Minor. The mission was to study the dead space phenomena and the local legends of an ancient civilisation. What we quickly discovered was unexpected. The area was awash with pirates who made a living from expeditions such as ours. Selling second-hand state of the art science equipment and ships makes a lot of money, as does selling slaves that have special skills. Any crew member not having a resale value, though, would be marooned, as they were surplus to requirements."

"You were marooned then?" Alienbutt asked.

"How did you guess?" Stoney asked looking at Alienbutt.

"You were the entertainments officer. When things get rough it's the entertainment officer and the food vending technician that are the first to go."

"In that order too," Stoney added, laughing. "They kept the technician though, so I was marooned alone."

"So how did you escape and get here?" Alienbutt asked.

"I was marooned on the edge of dead space in a large asteroid. It was one of the alleged outposts of the ancient civilisation and had a breathable atmosphere in its hollow centre. I was an amateur archaeologist in my youth and so started hunting around the place in my boredom. The place was littered with items that I collected together. Most were of little use, but I found a few strange amulets. I then came across a large circle with strange carvings; it was hidden within a room beyond a rock fall. I don't know how but it activated and I found myself somewhere else. I was in a strange temple and the priests there didn't seem happy to see me."

"You found a portal? Where's the temple?" Alienbutt asked excitedly.

"The temple is an evil place, Alienbutt. The priests sacrifice anyone who isn't a believer; I barely escaped with my life. They are a death cult and have spent  thousands of years trying to activate that portal so they could conquer space and escape some weird curse that means only a few can leave the desolate planet they live upon. When I first arrived they thought I was their ticket to escape. It was because I was wearing one of the strange amulets I found, around my neck. It was a holy symbol to them and must have made them nervous of killing me. I will not tell you of the events that happened, but finally I managed to steal a ship and escape them. I travelled across the universe to put as much space between them and me as possible."

"So there is a gateway for me to get back home, I just need to get past the mad priests to get to it," Alienbutt said with a smile. "Where do I find that temple, Stoney?"

"It's more than mad priests," Stoney said sadly. "I travelled for twenty years, crossed three war zones and even then there are no guarantees you can open the portal and make it take you to the right place. It's over a hundred years since I made that journey and I have no intention of trying to get back. I'm old now and live in a place of peace. My life is good. I'm not going back home to Earth and a war zone for anyone."

Alienbutt sat in his room. The news he had obtained from Stoney of a way home had raised his hopes, but the old man had refused to take him. There was also the fact it was a twenty year journey; by the time he got back the war would be over. He was stuck here or doomed to arrive back far too late. The trader would be leaving the frog planet later that day and had offered to take Alienbutt with him to start a new life as a trader. Knowing that the frog people didn't really want him here, he had accepted. He stood struggling to fasten his belt one-handed when Isme walked in. Without a word she walked over and fastened the buckle.

"How will you ever manage when you can't even fasten your own belt?" she asked, turning around and picking up the handguns from the bed to pass to him.

"I'll have to learn, Princess," he said with a smile.

"I've been thinking about what Stoney has said about your

way home," she said with a shy smile. "The two of you have overlooked something."

Alienbutt looked at her blankly. "And what would that be, my Princess?"

"Neither our people nor Stoney has a ship that can travel at this light speed your ships do. You have two damaged ships that, once repaired, can travel that fast."

Alienbutt stood without moving as her words sank in and then he grinned. "And Frank and Kirk had almost repaired Wickede's ship while we waited to leave."

"You should go talk again to Stoney and offer a trade. I'm sure even a damaged light speed drive could get you a map to this temple you seek."

"And the weaponry on that Federation ship will be enough to kick open the doors when I get there," Alienbutt added with a smile.


Stoney sat and looked at Alienbutt as he finished making his offer. The possibility of a light speed drive was one worth thinking about, he decided. Still, he was a trader and needed to haggle to get the best deal.

"The trouble with your offer is no one here knows how to fix the drive or even what is wrong with it."

"But Frank left his workshop intact; industrial replicators, spare parts and a diagnostic computer to tell us what to do. He said the jump had burnt out all the C.P. relays and master control switch," Alienbutt pressed excitedly.

"There is still a little problem, Alienbutt," Stoney said, and looked pointedly at Alienbutt's missing hand. "How much can a one-handed warrior do?"

Alienbutt smiled. "I've been thinking about that too, and I'm going to ask my dad to give me a hand with that particular problem."

29

# CHAPTER 4

## Waiting for Lightspeed.

### INTERSTELLAR NEWS CHANNEL 9.
### NEWS FLASH.

In business news it has been reported that the Loc Ness theme park, Olde Scotland on the planet Earth has gone into liquidation. Reports from an official spokesman blame a lack of off-world tourists because of travel restrictions as being responsible for its downturn in fortune. The family of Trescoplaphones imported from the ocean planet of Sebrine to play the part of Nessie after the original beasts were killed are now at the centre of a bidding war with the J.O. School Dinners for Olde Britannia plc., favourite to buy them. A spokesman said they had come up with a recipe to create a new range of Nessie battered twizzlers. A spokesman for the theme park would only say that they are looking into all possible options for the Trescolaphones but the Nessie twizzlers did sound a real tasty snack.

Loc Ness Olde Scotland theme park had been a great success since the land was purchased. It had been the last independent state on Earth before being bought out by Galactic Theme Parks plc. as the ancient nation went into liquidation. The new owners then began wide-scale eviction of its people and enforced strict copyright laws on its historic products such as whisky, leading to the use of the historic Irish spelling being used for all spirits not produced inside the theme park. With the ongoing war the theme park has become the largest victim of the economic squeeze.

Kaela was the youngest Major in the Outer System's Marine Corps, He had started his career as a weapons technician just before the war broke out. Too young for active service, he had learnt all about building and servicing small arms until he was old enough to join the infantry. Over the following two years he had seen action on a dozen worlds, protecting the giant ore facilities in some of the bloodiest battles of the war. His reputation for getting the job done had gained him a transfer to the Marine Corps last year as a sergeant-at-arms. His skill, combined with the short life expectancy of the new position, had seen him gain rapid promotion. The job was simple; they had to protect the internal cargo bay shield generators from boarding parties of Federation battle droids on the giant transport vessels ferrying precious ore for the construction of new ships. Since taking over command his team was the only one to never lose any cargo to the Federation snatch squads. If the cargo bay shield generator was knocked out, Federation ships would use transporter beams to remove entire cargo units to their ships, before falling back with their valuable trophy. With the war dragging on, the ore facilities and the precious goods had become vital to the war efforts of both sides.

The giant transporters left the mining facilities in large convoys and headed out into space. The transport ships were too large to be manoeuvrable and had to clear the asteroid belt of Ashia Minor before they could jump to light speed and head for the Ick shipyards, full of their precious cargo. The convoys had to slowly negotiate their way through a no-man's land, where the waiting Federation fleets would pounce. Intense battles would take place with every convoy that left, as the Federation tried to first steal and then destroy the cargo. Once able to jump to light speed their escort ships would be left behind to return to defending the mining facilities while the transporters would be safe from further attack and soon reach the safety of Ick Space.

The red alert had already sounded as the battle outside the ship raged, the Federation seeking to land a boarding craft onto the transporter's hull so the droids could cut through and enter the ship. Kaela stood waiting with his fifty-strong team. Even with the reduced onboard gravity of the ship, the Marine battle armour was heavy and uncomfortable. From the large gravity boots, the chest armour with its life support system, to the combat helmet, the battle suit weighed twice that of the soldier inside it. When switched to combat mode the suit's armour became weightless but the drain on the power pack was such that it was kept switched off till the last possible moment. Losing power during a battle could prove troublesome and often deadly for the suit's owner. A six-foot brightly coloured slow-moving statue made an easy target for the battle droids.

The loud metallic clashes sounding up and down the ship signalled that the first of the boarding craft had connected to the transporter hull. This was quickly followed by a high-pitched screech as the droids began to drill through the armoured plating of the hull, seeking to enter.

"OK boys and girls, it's power up time," ordered Kaela. His unit sprang into action as they switched on their armour. They moved into position, each knowing their job and where they needed to be. Reaching back over his shoulder he unclipped one of his two great pulse rifles, as just up ahead in the vast hall of the ship's cargo bay sparks began to spray down from the ship's hull, signalling that the first of the droids was almost through. Eight hundred giant cargo units' containers were the prize they were after, each one containing ten thousand tons of refined metal ore.

A large circular section of the hull fell to the floor with a giant crash, quickly followed by the first of the battle droids leaping down into the ship's interior. The first droids were cut down as his team opened fire. Within moments more sections of the hull fell in and the battle was joined in earnest as hundreds of battle droids swarmed into the hold.

Ponnfarr flew through the battle. The giant transport ships that his squadron were providing escort to were already being swarmed over by the small droid boarding crafts; thousands had been launched from the Federation troop carriers. Most would be destroyed by his fighter ships before they reached their destination, but hundreds always got past them. Meanwhile the squadron of frigates under his command engaged the Federation capital ships in an intense fire-fight where survival became more a matter of luck than skill. Ponnfarr cast a last quick look at the transporters. Many of the boarding craft had already attached themselves to the giant hulls. He knew the droids inside would soon be spilling into the giant transporters and the fighting inside would be much worse.

"This is Ponnfarr to all fleet. Concentrate all fire on those battle-cruisers; I want them all taken out fast," he ordered, and instantly intense fire fell on the Federation capital ships. He had only one other Fo'c'sle ship in his command. The rest of the squadron was made up of Outer System militia and crews that had changed sides after Wickede's return with the cure for coffee. While not of the same skill as his comrades in the elite Ick squadron, they were learning quickly, and eager to prove themselves. He knew the battle would be short but brutal, as within twenty minutes the first of the transporters would make the jump to light speed. That would be the signal for the Federation Battle cruisers to target the transport ships, trying to disable or destroy them to prevent their escape, as chances of stealing more cargo would then come to an end. His job was to ensure as few of the Federation battle-cruisers as possible were still a threat when the transporters became targets. The marines inside the transporters would give their lives to protect their cargo, and he would ensure that none fell to the battle-cruisers' lethal firepower.

Major Kaela had unclipped his second rifle, and now with one in each hand was been slowly forced back towards the shield generator by sheer numbers of droids. Moving between the giant containers that acted as cover, his squad was inflicting massive damage on the battle droid numbers. Down the aisle between two rows of containers, a group of over twenty droids had formed up and were marching down, sending out a devastating barrage of fire towards his men; three were already down. Checking the clips in his rifles he waited. One of his men threw an anti-droid mine down the aisle. As it exploded he stepped into the middle of the aisle and opened fire, cutting down the droids not destroyed by the mine. The intense close quarters fighting within the hold was dependent on teamwork and each member of his team acting without hesitation, even if it meant their life.

The battle had been raging for twenty minutes before he finally received the thirty-second notice that the ship would be jumping to light speed. Quickly he took cover behind one of the five-thousand tonne containers that were magnetically welded to the hold floor and prepared to magnetise his boots. This would lock his suit rigid to stand like an immovable statue. Looking around quickly he saw his squad had already prepared for the jump and stood rigid. With seconds to spare he locked his suit.

The ship made the jump to light speed and everything within the hold turned to chaos. Within the giant hold of the transporter there were no buffering shields to fully protect those inside from the G-force of a jump to light speed as there was in other ships. Without the battle suits and warning of the jump his squad would have been lifted off their feet and slammed into any fixed object in their path with the force of about thirty gravities. Through gritted teeth at the pressure still exerted on them Major Kaela watched as the invading droids were lifted into the air to fly past, crashing into each other and the containers. Small explosions were seen as the droid units power packs ruptured. Anything not locked down was lifted up to end up smashed to scrap as it flew through the air towards the back of the ship. The droid attack was over in an instant, the entire invading force destroyed. The droid landing craft were stripped from the outside of the hull by the force of the acceleration and for a split second the transporter faced being ripped apart as the hold depressurised, then the inner atmosphere shields kicked in, preventing the air escaping. Within ten seconds it was over and the gravity within the transporter hold returned to normal. Releasing the magnetism of the boots and unlocking the joints of the battle suit so he could move again, Kaela walked into the aisle and looked down to see the great pile of wrecked droids at the far end of the ship. Bonus parts towards the war effort, his Sergeant would always say. To Kaela it just signified he had survived to do it all again next time.

"OK, you know the drill. Sweep the hold for any droid that still works, then it's time for dinner. Sergeant, give the order for our service droids to get to work and get the hull patched before those shields fail."

Ponnfarr watched as the Federation ships withdrew. The convoy was safely away with the destruction of just one of the twelve transporters. A small number of containers had been transported from a couple of the others but the marines had again held out well in protecting the shield generators. His squadron had formed up as they prepared to return to the refinery and the next convoy, which would be going out within a couple of days.

"Captain Ponnfarr, there's an incoming message from Commander Kali, secure Fo'c'sle channel," his communications officer said, half turning in his chair.

"Put it through to me here," he ordered as he sat at the pilot's chair. Quickly he read the message and smiled. "Order Gwidion to take over returning the escort. He's in command of the unit until my return."

The communications officer grinned at Ponnfarr. "I'm sure he's gonna thank you for the promotion, Captain."

Grinning back Ponnfarr replied; "Tell him it's only temporary until we find someone better."

Ponnfarr sat back in the chair and waited. Within moments of his communications officer sending the message, Gwidion was demanding to speak to him.

"All right Ponnfarr, what're you doing trying to palm your responsibilities onto me?" he asked.

"I have new orders and have to leave now," Ponnfarr replied. "We've found our lost lamb and Kali wants the best we've got to go and get her."

"So why are you going? Does she need cannon fodder to act as a distraction?" Gwidion asked, laughing.

Ponnfarr grinned. "You'd better hope not or you'll never get the money I owe you."

"What? You're actually going to pay me when you get back?" Gwidion said, surprised.

"Probably not, but you can live in hope, stay alive."

"Make sure you leave your money with Kali before the attack starts and don't do anything stupid, as the drinks are on you when you get back."

"I don't have any money till we get paid, you know that Gwidion," Ponnfarr lied.

"So you didn't win two hundred credits from Frandar last night then?" Gwidion asked, already knowing the answer.

"O.K. I'll buy the drinks when I get back. You're taking the food out of my..." Ponnfarr began defensively.

"I know, your poor starving mum's mouth. Stay safe and give 'em hell," cut in Gwidion, not letting him finish.

# CHAPTER 5

## Rescue.

INTERSTELLAR NEWS CHANNEL 9.
NEWS FLASH.

The Coffee Houses today announced they are expecting a bumper crop of coffee beans. Experimental weather manipulation on a number of the production planets is expected to raise harvest levels by an estimated fifteen per cent. Extra security will be placed at all facilities ready for the immediate transport of the first part of the crop in two weeks. Coffee House scientists also reported a breakthrough in treatment of the addictive aspect of the bean and hope to be rolling out treatment to the Inner Systems over the next few months. Rumours that the Ick have found a cure have been dismissed as desperate propaganda and a last throw of the dice by the crumbling empire. Initial trials of the new treatment are showing positive signs that coffee addiction could be consigned to history. Arabica Medical, a subsidiary of the Coffee House conglomerate who are developing the treatment are the universal leader in medical science. Working with their sister company Cultivar transport who distribute coffee to all areas of the Inner Systems, we should see the treatment rapidly rolled out once it is cleared by Arusha Medical, the Federal standards' boards of medical research.

Morgan had worked at the estates of General Jee on the planet AV32 for many years and had risen to be deputy commander of the estates' security. With the sudden departure of the General less than a week before, life for the estate staff was now returning to a more peaceful normality. Or it would have been if Morgan hadn't just received the message before her. Within two hours a fleet of Fo'c'sle ships would be jumping out of light speed above the planet to rescue the prisoner held in the basement cells of the main house. The identity of the prisoner was top secret and she had only confirmed who it was a few days before and reported her findings to Snoodgrass, her true employer. State of the art security and defence systems on the estates would be able to slow down the Fo'c'sle long enough for a relief fleet of Federation warships to arrive. The fact that a rescue attempt was even being staged showed how important the prisoner was. For her to be ordered to blow her ten year cover getting close to the General left no doubt how highly the Ick wanted her back. Morgan, codenamed Whiff, was one of Snoodgrass's highest placed spies and would have her work cut out to disable the security systems and spring the prisoner in time for the Fo'c'sle's arrival. She had been recruited into the life of a secret agent by a kindly old monk of the Order of Sung the One-eyed Lama. She had gone to the Temple as a child seeking refuge after her family had been killed in coffee riots on her home world. One of Snoodgrass's biggest secrets was that the religious cult was a front for many of his agents. It had temples on most worlds in the Federation. The monks were famous for their acts of charity, but much less famous for being some of the best spies, information gatherers and recruitment agents within the Federation.

Destroying the message, she walked out of her office and headed for the staff sleeping quarters. When the General wasn't on the estates a squad of just twenty security personnel remained behind. Half of those would be out patrolling the vast estates and were not expected back for over three days. This left just ten for her to deal with. With half of those off duty and asleep in their quarters she headed to deal with them first to ensure they wouldn't wake up. Removing a small capsule from her belt, she opened the door to the sleeping quarters, pressed a button on top of the capsule and threw it onto the nearest bed. Quickly closing the door she walked on towards the security office. The gas in the capsule was fast acting and the five guards would be in a coma within a minute. She had spent years with these people and would prefer to keep the death toll by her own hand down, at least, . She very much doubted that those arriving soon would be too interested in keeping casualties down, but it made her feel better.

Morgan walked into the security office. Two more of the guards sat lounging in their chairs. They looked over as she entered before returning their attention to a film they were watching on a monitor.

"What's up, Morgan, are you bored already?" asked one, his attention already returned to the film. Morgan didn't reply as she pulled a small tranquillizer gun out of her holster, and both guards were unconscious at their post before they even realised there was a threat. The General was paranoid about assassination so the guards were only allowed tranquillizer guns. As deputy commander of security she did have keys to an extensive armoury though, where she could get any number of other guns that could make large explosions happen or just put holes into people. Both guards sat slumped in their chairs and would normally remain that way for the next twenty-four hours. Knowing what was happening within two hours' time, Morgan doubted they would ever wake up. She moved over to the main security computer and placed a small disc into the drive. Within ten minutes of it activating the virus on the disk would shut down the estates' defence systems. Checking the systems' overview she saw that two of the remaining guards were down in the basement with the prisoner, while the last one was on the top floor. With a last look at the two sleeping guards Morgan headed out of the room. She would have to dispose of the one on the roof first.

Grommit sat on the floor, her legs crossed. Her left arm itched below the medi-patch that was healing the shattered bones in her wrist. After each beating her brother would ensure her injuries were treated, ready for the next round of punishment inflicted on her. For almost a week now, Jee hadn't been down to give her a beating. She didn't know why this was but was thankful for the respite and a chance to fully heal. The two guards that he had left seemed to spend much of their time watching programs on a monitor screen. They were never rotated with any of the other guards and took it in turns sleeping on a small bunk. Twice a day a robot would enter to bring them food and drink, and the meagre rations that she was allowed. When the door into the chamber opened neither guard bothered to look up, so they didn't see the female guard who walked in through the doorway. Grommit saw the robot that delivered the meals beyond the door, its head unit severed. The new arrival was ignored until one of the guards finally looked up. Surprised, he started to rise, a look of confusion on his face. The female guard leapt forward unexpectedly, a cyber-sword in each hand. The four-foot laser blades materialised out of the handles as she swung her arms in a vicious arc, the blades slicing through both guards, who fell dead before they realised what was happening. Grommit was impressed by the speed of the new arrival; the cyber-sword was a highly skilled weapon, one that only an expert would attempt to use against armed guards. When armed it had a four-foot blade that was lethal in close combat, slicing through even armoured steel. When not in use the laser blade retracted into the handle for easy storage and could be clipped to a belt. The newcomer ran over to the cell control panel and shut down the energy shield that kept Grommit imprisoned.

"Move it, girl, we've only got a minute before the second level of security kicks in," she shouted, already heading back for the door, the swords still held at the ready. Grommit jumped up and ran for the door. As she reached it she heard metallic grinding from behind her. Turning to look back into the chamber where she had been held, she saw circular sections of the floor sliding back and robotic infantry units rising up in cylinders from the floor.

"We need to move before those things start to activate," Morgan said, grabbing Grommit by the arm. "There's over fifty of those things in there and this door won't hold them for long. We need to get to the armoury."

Grommit stepped through the door while Morgan pressed the button to shut it before placing a small dial onto the control unit that shorted out the circuit in a shower of sparks. Turning, without a further word she headed up the passage to the surface.

Three dreadnoughts and seven cruisers jumped out of light speed above the planet AV23. Immediately they moved into position in orbit and began firing at targets on the planet, taking out known defensive positions. Commander Kali sat in the command chair of the lead dreadnought watching the barrage aimed planet-side.

"Commander, the estate security shields are disabled as Commander Snoodgrass promised," her technical officer informed her after completing a scan of the planet's surface.

"Send down the away team and make sure you keep

scanning the system for any sign of Federation ships. Now let's hope Snoodgrass's spy Whiff is as good as he claims and this runs to plan. I don't want a stand-up battle with any relief fleet."

"Commander, we have five battle cruisers moving from orbit around the planets moon, E.T.A. four minutes," reported a young ensign seated at the weapons console.

"The general left something for us to play with, how thoughtful. Order Cyborgpirate to lead the cruisers and engage. Best to let him play while we await the away team; all fighters on standby," she replied calmly. "Now could I have a nice cuppa tea while we wait?"

The away team materialised outside the main building on General Jee's estates. Killashandra quickly looked around, taking stock of her surroundings. In the distance a column of smoke rose into the sky where the Fo'c'sle ships had targeted other buildings on the estate. The other ten members of the team had spread into a defensive circle waiting for her orders. She walked over to her number two, Ponnfarr.

"Let's leave a couple out here. The rest of us will enter the building and search for Grommit and this spy."

Ponnfarr nodded and got up from his crouching position. Killashandra cursed inwardly, as now she would have to start looking up at the squad of towering soldiers again. It was difficult to give orders when she was on a level with their armpits.

As they approached the doorway to the house they heard gunfire and explosions from inside. Two of the soldiers raced forward and quickly placed small charges on the door. The away team all moved to either side of the doorway as the charges went off, removing the doors from the frame; before the dust and smoke cleared they raced through. Flipping down a screen on their helmets they moved through the dust-filled and smoky interior using infrared to pierce the haze of smoke and dust. Checking a small screen on her wrist as she turned around, Killashandra picked up two life readings off down a corridor to the left. Using hand signals she indicated the way the team should go.

Grommit and Morgan lay behind a small wall of a fountain in an enclosed garden forecourt. The robotic infantry had them pinned down, and it would not be long before they started to outflank them. Morgan had picked up an assault rifle each from the armoury and the two had fought a running battle with the robots as they came up from the underground chamber, but now their luck had run out.

"So was there more to your plan than just getting us topside?" Grommit asked as she placed the final clip into her rifle.

"Your friends were supposed to be here to meet us." Morgan rose up over the wall and fired her rifle, hitting a robot that fell over backwards, its head ripped apart. "On the bright side the sun's out, so stop bitching and let's work on our tans while we wait for them. Sung knows you could do with a bit of sun. You're really pale and a bit of colour will make you look less like you just got busted out of a prison cell," she continued, ducking back down as the robots returned fire, causing shards of stone to shower over them from the wall behind them.

"Sunbathing? Without any sunblock?" Grommit gasped in disgust as she rolled to her right and took out a robot that was moving to get around the side of them. "Do you know how bad that ages the skin, and pale skin is the look to have this season," she said with a grin as she rolled back behind the wall. "It's called prisoner chic."

"Stop yer bloody beauty tips and get ya heads down!" shouted a voice from the balcony above, before a sustained volley of gunfire erupted, cutting into the advancing robot. As the echoes of the gunfire began to fade two figures jumped over the balcony to land lightly beside the two women. Ponnfarr stood in the pool of the fountain and reached into a pouch on his belt. With a fluid motion he threw a small object that burst into blue light as it flew in a spinning arc to slice through the remaining robots.

"Years out of the arena but I still got the moves. The undefeated champion of Heeter racing to your rescue, ladies," he said as the glowing object flew back to his hand, its light turning out as he caught it.

"You want a ride home?" asked the other who had jumped down with a grin.

"What took you so long, Killashandra?" Grommit asked as she began to get to her feet, then saw movement from behind her friend as one of the robot infantry rose up. It was damaged, but still operational. Alerted by Grommit's warning glance Killashandra spun around and leapt at the robot. With one hand she reached up and grabbed the top of the robot's chest plate and pulled herself up to stare eye to robotic eye with the robot. She rammed her helmeted head twice into the robotic eye. The metallic body began to topple backwards, and as it did, she pulled out her handgun and fired into the gap between the chest plate and neck. Jumping clear she stared down at the now ruined robot.

"These helmets would come in handy down on Hardstool on a Friday night. I wonder how our champion here would fair in a real bust-up without his fancy toys." Raising her wrist to speak into her wrist-com she grinned at Grommit. "Killashandra to Kali, we got twelve to beam up."

Ponnfarr, still standing in the fountain, shrugged. "Why have toys if you don't play with them?"

# CHAPTER 6

## Threats of Violence.

### INTERSTELLAR NEWS CHANNEL 9.
### NEWS FLASH.

Early news on the cure for coffee addiction is showing promising results. It appears a simple psychoactive stimulant added to the plant as it grows removes all symptoms of addiction but still allows the universe to enjoy its favourite beverage. Coffee House scientists are heralding the trial as a total success and will be adding the stimulant biologically to this year's crop. Arusha Medical has cleared the treatment to be distributed across the Inner Systems, after it passed all its safety checks.

In other news the Senate today gave the go-ahead for the formation of new cyborg battle units. Experiments will start on volunteer prisoners deemed to be a threat to the Federation with no chance of redemption to normal society. The new force will be used to replace troops in the most dangerous battle arenas. Robusta Military will lead the project, working with Timor Security, who oversees the prison systems.

Nifty opened her eyes and looked up at a white ceiling and decided that these definitely weren't her quarters, as she had painted them a pale pink with large yellow flowers while she waited for the time the Book of Ick said she should act. Hearing a soft regular beeping she turned her head and saw a medical screen showing someone's heart rate. Sitting up she discovered a small clip on the index finger of her right hand so removed it. The heart rate on the machine went into a flat line and a red button began to flash. Swinging her legs off the bed to stand up, she had a flash of memory, a metallic cat face. A stranger in a medical uniform ran into the room and stopped when he saw her standing by the bed.

"Please could you get back into bed. You've been ill for quite a while and you will be feeling weak," he said, walking over, a look of concern on his face.

Nifty sat back down as memories began to resurface; the attack by the robotic Mr Fluffy, and Blackarachnia coming to help her before someone shot her. Her hand went to her chest. Feeling nothing, she pulled forward the front of the gown she wore and looked in disbelief at the scar that wasn't there. She looked up at the stranger, an unspoken question on her lips.

"You came in close to death, but we managed to heal the wounds," he supplied the answer before she asked, then continued: "If you give me a moment I will put a call out for the bounty hunter that you came in with."

"Blackarachnia is here? Thank god for that," she said with relief.

"No, Miss, I meant Hydroponic."

Nifty grabbed the medic by the front of his tunic and spoke dangerously low, pulling him in close so they were face to face.

"I don't know any Hydroponic. Now where's my bloody husband?"

The medic tried to pull back, amazed and terrified by the

strength the woman had, and the fury that was suddenly in her eyes. He knew of Blackarachnia; working on the bounty hunter's space station how could he not? But he truly feared for the bounty hunter's health if his wife was to get hold of him for not being here when she woke up.

Duke Ramboe stood explaining the events since she had arrived at the station to Nifty. Even though she was restrained, he was standing well back. Hydroponic sat on a bed at the other side of the medical ward close to the door, absently rolling up a cigarette, while six security officers stood to attention. All were wishing they weren't on duty and trying hard to look anything but menacing after seeing what had happened to the previous squad that had first responded to the distress call from the medical ward. Smashed equipment still littered the room and the blood splatter hadn't been cleaned up yet. The security teams on the station prided themselves on being ready for anything, dealing with the often drunken bounty hunters, who were liable to start a fight just for fun. They were trained in stopping fights quickly, but nothing had prepared them for dealing with this patient. Never before had it taken two full squads to subdue one person, and they were thankful that she had just woken up from a coma and was still weak, or they would have needed at least another two squads. Finally Duke Ramboe finished talking and looked at Nifty, waiting for her response. At least the look of murder had disappeared from her eyes, he thought.

"So you're telling me you allowed my husband to walk out of here in that state of mind?" The words were spoken with quiet menace.

"I think that's a little unfair, Nifty, you know how difficult Blackarachnia can be," responded Duke Ramboe defensively. "Now if you promise to not attack anyone else I will release the restraints."

The security team took a step back while Hydroponic got ready to race for the exit. Nifty took a deep breath before nodding.

"There's one last thing I need to tell you first. The rescue mission for Wickede was a success, apart from one thing; Alienbutt didn't make it back. We think that the news coupled with your injury is what sent Blackarachnia on his rampage," Duke Ramboe said awkwardly, taking a step further back.

"If you do not release these bloody restraints and get me a ship I will tear this station apart, and you really don't want to know where I will shove the pieces," responded Nifty very slowly. A crash from behind Duke Ramboe made him spin around. Looking down he saw one of the security guards had fainted, while the remaining five looked terrified. Looking over at Hydroponic he saw the bounty hunter had lit his cigarette and was inspecting his fingertips as if he had never seen them before. With an evil grin, Duke Ramboe turned back to Nifty.

"Hydroponic has a ship and knows Blackarachnia's hunting methods better than anyone, so you have got a ship and a guide to go with it."

Hydroponic's head shot up. "What?"

Duke Ramboe continued, ignoring the bounty hunter. "Once the Doctor gives you a clean bill of health I'll turn off the restraints and you're free to go."

"Well, could you please get the doctor in here now, before I get bored of waiting," Nifty said in a sweet voice that was even more chilling.

Duke Ramboe indicated to one of the guards to get the doctor and then turned and walked out. Hydroponic jumped down from the bed and fell in beside the bounty hunters' leader.

"Now you listen. I'm a civilian, you can't make me go on

any missions," he declared as they got outside. Duke Ramboe stopped and glared down at Hydroponic before he smiled.

"We're at war and even if you didn't hold a valid bounty hunter licence I would conscript you. You go, or I transfer you to the infantry on the swamp world of Dreadmarsh. That poor sweet girl wants to go find her husband and there is no way in Sung that I'm standing in her way. Am I making myself clear?"

"My licence expired over five years ago, so don't try pulling that one," Hydroponic protested.

"I renewed it the day you got back," Duke Ramboe announced with an evil grin.

"That's illegal and against Federation law," replied Hydroponic, shocked at Duke Ramboe's blatant law breaking.

"So report me to the Senate." Duke Ramboe slapped him on the shoulder, smiling. "You will act as a guide to Nifty or I'll make your life impossible." He walked off leaving a crestfallen Hydroponic muttering about sneaky underhand tactics.

Guerick Tackful didn't believe in luck. It was all down to planning and training. So he was at a loss to understand how he had managed to end up being held prisoner. After his run in with Blackarachnia, he had spent a week in a medi-tank recovering from his injuries before heading back to the dreadnought to hunt for clues as to where his target may have gone. It was here that his luck had run out and things had gone downhill.

He had beamed aboard what should have been an empty ship; he had seen the mangled armoured suit of the mysterious Mr Fluffy, and a scan of the ship showed no life signs. With him he had taken an away team of four, each man a highly dependable veteran of many hunts and battles. In the cargo bay they had found the crates they had delivered empty. The next surprise had been the crew of Blackarachnia's ship. They had moved around like robotic zombies, unaware of any events around them as they went about their tasks. The first crew member they had come across they had killed. It was only then that they had seen the black box embedded into the base of the skull. Guerick had seen mind control devices before but never anything like that.

It was just after this that they had encountered the mysterious Mr Fluffy. He was very much alive and had built a new battle suit from the parts they had delivered. He stood at almost seven feet of armoured steel, shaped roughly like a human, but the head was that of a cat. Within moments it had killed his men, before turning its attention to him. The suit had some sort of shielding that made his guns useless. Still, Guerick had stood his ground, emptying his guns of ammunition at him. Mr Fluffy had stood still, purring as the bullets bounced from his suit before he struck with stunning speed. He had avoided the first lunge, and tried to radio his ship for aid but couldn't get through.

Knocked senseless by the next attack, he had awoken in an energy cell within the science laboratory. He had watched as the zombie crew had brought in his own crew from his own ship and installed the control devices in each one. Guerick had no morals, but knew that what was happening here was not good. He knew without doubt he was watching the start of something that was truly evil. Killing and murder were one thing but to make people into zombified slaves was just going too far even for him to take.

After seeing the final member of his crew fitted with the black box, Mr Fluffy had come to see him and he had been given a choice. He could be fitted with a control device or he could work for Mr Fluffy willingly. Guerick had inwardly smiled, knowing that a chance to escape would come his way, so he had chosen the second option. He would agree to work for Mr Fluffy and make his move the first chance he got. That was before Mr Fluffy had added his insurance policy by injecting him with nanoprobes that would attack and destroy his body from the inside if he ever tried to betray his new master. Then just to hammer home the point, he had surgically implanted a nano drive into his brain and nano camera into his eye so he would be able to record and see whatever Guerick did. Guerick was in trouble, but he was alive and he tried to convince himself he just had a new employer. He failed in convincing himself and cursed his bad luck.

Nifty walked aboard Hydroponic's ship. It was much smaller than the ships she was used to and looked as though it was about ready for the scrap yard from her first glance. Blackarachnia had taught her to look beyond the obvious and on a closer inspection she could see how hard Hydroponic had worked to make the ship appear a pile of junk, when in fact it was heavily armoured, packing state of the art weapons, and she doubted it would be slow or sluggish. She found Hydroponic in the small flight room checking the ship's computer. He looked over as she walked in.

"I've cleared the second room on the right for you, first one's the bathroom. Sorry, but the ship doesn't run to separate facilities," he said gruffly.

Nifty looked back down the short corridor towards the doors he had indicated.

"Could I start by saying thank you and get it out of the way?" She asked, turning back to him.

"You can, but thanks work better with a large reward attached," he grumbled, not looking up from the computer monitor until a packet of cigars landed in front of him.

"Duke Ramboe said these are your favourites, but you

smoke them in your room or you'll be eating them."

Hydroponic looked up to see her smiling, taking the sting out of the words and nodded, picking up the packet and placing it in his shirt pocket.

"Sounds fair, you seem an almost reasonable person when not threatening to rip space stations apart. Now we've got the rules out of the way and you know where you're sleeping, get your kit. We leave as soon as you're ready. I got news of a likely Spider sighting so want to get there before it gets too cold."

"I've got what I need, so let's get going, but we're not going looking for Blackarachnia straight away," Nifty replied, sitting down in the co-pilots chair.

"What?" a confused Hydroponic asked, looking over at Nifty's smiling face.

"I took some time to read a bit of Duke Ramboe's copy of the Book of Ick. Let's go fly around a bit until it's time to go see Snoodgrass. I know when and where Blackarachnia will be, so chasing after where he has already been seems pointless unless you like looking at dead people."

Hydroponic shook his head. "And when will it be time to see Snoodgrass?" he asked.

"I'll let you know," Nifty said sweetly.

"Are you always this cryptic or are you trying extra hard for some strange female reason that I'll never understand?" Hydroponic asked, beginning his pre-flight checks.

# CHAPTER 7

## A Fathers Helping Hand.

INTERSTELLAR NEWS CHANNEL 9.
NEWS FLASH.

As the unofficial truce in the Outer Systems enters its second month, there have been calls from sections of the Senate for formal peace talks. Senator Gralswige moved quickly to rubbish such calls, stating that while there had been no large scale battles, Ick backed infiltration units had been extremely active, carrying out terror attacks often dressed as E.D.F. personnel. Other terror attacks have included the destruction of General Jee's personal estates on the planet AV23, which he had converted to treat soldiers of both sides injured on the front line. When asked, the General's press secretary reported the loss of life was being counted in the thousands. The estate had clear marking and signals to show it was a hospital facility and had no defences. The attack had left the General visibly shocked at the depths of terror the Ick would stoop to.

Alienbutt sat looking at the metallic hand on the table before him. The synthetic covering had been removed to reveal the skeletal frame. Stoney had removed the hand from Alienbutt's dead cyborg father's body and cleaned it up ready to be fitted.

"Well boy, do you know how to do this?" Stoney asked, placing a metallic wrist tube next to the hand. "That's the cradle it attaches to. That connection array inside that tube looks like it will be painful to fit to your arm."

Alienbutt inspected the inside of the tube that would be placed over his wrist. "I need to scan the connectors to make sure they aren't damaged. The medical files cover how to connect it to my arm. The replicator can produce the medi-nano bots that will connect the nerves and tendons to the cradle."

"Are you sure this is going to work?" Stoney asked, looking unconvinced.

"Computer says so. How's the work on the ship going?" Alienbutt asked, changing the subject. A team of the frog people's technicians had accompanied them to help fix the damage to the outside of Wickede's ship and transfer any items of use to it.

"They say another week before the ship's spaceworthy. The light speed drives will be ready soon after. You sure we can't fix one of the jump drives? It'd make things a lot easier for you."

"We can make the parts for the control units, but the whole program to make them work is fried and there's no backup," Alienbutt said as he lifted a small cover on the cradle and connected a cable from the computer. As lights began to blink on the cradle's control unit he began to remove the bandage from his arm.

"Won't you need some sort of pain medication, Alienbutt?" Stoney asked, looking concerned.

"Don't think so," Alienbutt said as he finished removing the bandage, and then picking up a syringe, injected a green glowing liquid into a small opening on the control panel. "That's the medi-nanos loaded up; it's ready to go."

"Did you read all the instructions on how to fit this cradle? I'm sure you need pain relief," Stoney pressed, concern evident in his voice.

"Don't worry, Stoney, I read all the technical stuff last night, I'm doing it all correctly." Alienbutt placed the cradle onto his arm, smiling.

"What about reading about patient care?" Stoney still pressed, looking worried.

"You worry too much." With that he pressed a button on the computer to start the meld of cradle to his arm. After a second he began to scream and jumped to his feet, just before he passed out.

"I knew it, Alienbutt, you needed pain relief," Stoney said to the unconscious Alienbutt.

Alienbutt opened his eyes, not moving he realised something was weird. For a start the room was moving in a strange way; the walls had never rippled before, he was certain. A face appeared above him and smiled reassuringly. After a moment Alienbutt recognised that it was Stoney.

"Are you back with us this time? Man you had me worried," Stoney said. "I thought you'd never wake up."

"What happened?" Alienbutt asked, confused.

"You went to attach your hand without pain relief and passed out before you could add the nano stimulant. Good job I was here or you would be dead," Stoney answered

Alienbutt raised his new hand so it was before his face and looked at the skeletal metallic hand. Wiggling the fingers, he was relieved to see them move as he wanted. "How long have

57

I been out?" he asked, sitting up. As he did the world around him gave another ripple as it adjusted to his new position. "And what's wrong with my vision? It's all wonky."

Stoney looked away before he answered. "Over a week. I've been real worried about you, Alienbutt. After you passed out I had to act quick to find out what to give you, and, well, my eyes aren't as young as they used to be. In my haste I misread a couple of quantities. I gave you a slight overdose on the pain killers."

"Never had a reaction like that to pain killers before, and for it to still be in my system." Alienbutt looked down at his arm and noticed that the entire arm was encased in metal up to the shoulder. He threw a look at Stoney, the question not needing to be asked.

"Like I said, my eyes are not as good as they used to be and I didn't see the dot, so instead of two point five mill of nano stimulant you got twenty five." Stoney paused and looked down at the floor. "Removing your whole arm was the only way to stop it killing you. We found the cyborg arm in the Federation ship's hold. It's brand new. It's a great bit of kit, Alienbutt, inbuilt smart chip control unit and targeting sensors. I was reading the instruction booklet waiting for you to wake up. It will be better than your..." He tailed off as he looked back up and saw the look on Alienbutt's face.

"You chopped off my arm?" Alienbutt asked, the fogginess in his head clearing as reality smashed through the drugged haze.

"Technically I just held you down. It was the frog physician that did the cutting," Stoney said defensively, stepping back. "There was another slight side effect too."

"Chopping off my arm is a slight side effect?" Alienbutt asked in disbelief.

"Bad choice of words. Compared to losing an arm, the

other effect is physically small in size," Stoney said, holding up one hand and indicating a small size with thumb and finger while nervously smiling.

Alienbutt got unsteadily to his feet as his vision again rippled. "I swear you had better just tell me before I do something we both regret." He grabbed the bed to steady himself. "And what the hell is up with my vision?"

"We had to replace an eye. I've read it's usual to have some visual disturbance for the first couple of hours after fitting a cyber-eye," Stoney said as he backed to the doorway.

"You had to replace my eye?! What the hell happened for me to lose an eye?" Alienbutt asked, disbelief taking over.

"It's not important, we fixed it. I do have some good news for you. Your ship's ready."

"It's a bloody good job. I'm running out of body parts for you all to remove," Alienbutt replied sarcastically. He noticed a metal cup next to the bed and reached out to pick it up. As the metallic fingers closed around the cup it crumpled under his touch, spilling the water. Alienbutt took a deep breath as he held onto control of himself.

"If I was you, I would use the other hand when you go to the toilet until it fine tunes itself on the grip pressure on that hand," Stoney suggested.

Alienbutt stood looking at the small Ick ship, barely more than a shuttle. He had to admit the frog people had done a great job of fixing it. The ship would be basic but it did have a light speed drive and now some weaponry and basic shields scavenged from the Federation scout ship. Also the extra equipment he had brought with him, that had not been needed as they had fixed the ship Wickede and Frank had escaped. in had saved a lot of time and work. The best thing was the case of thirty Ick torpedoes that would make his ship the most powerful craft in this area of space. With the light speed drive he should be able to get to the temple that Stoney had entered this dimension at within a couple of months. If the priests turned out to be unfriendly, then he had the means to change their minds about their attitude and [get them to] bugger off while he opened the gateway. How he would do this he didn't have a clue, but that would be a problem for when he arrived.

Stoney had told him of the strange priesthood that worshipped at the portal and would raid into the neighbouring systems to gather up sacrifices to throw into its grey mass, hoping to break the curse that held many of them trapped on their dying planet. Once that was done the High Priest would lead them in a war to convert all of space to their beliefs that anyone not of their race had to have their insides removed before being thrown into the void. Alienbutt had been shocked that priests would act like this, having only met those priests of the Book of Ick and an old priest of Sung the One Eyed Lama, when he was a child. Alienbutt thought having priests that ran around ordering people killed was a strange concept. They sounded more like politicians to him. Stoney had pointed out that in most cases the only difference between a politician and a priest was that a politician did horrible things for his own ends, while a priest would do horrible things for his own ends and then blame his god. Alienbutt decided that this longed-for religious war and sacrifice of people in the name of the cause by these priests was the second stupidest thing he had heard of. Still at number one, though, was the war over the ramblings of two dead crazy people over a coffee bean.

Alienbutt was brought out of his thoughts as Stoney came up and stood beside him. For a while neither spoke. It was three days since Alienbutt had awoken to discover the changes to his body and still Stoney refused to talk about the eye.

"The ship will be ready to leave in the morning, Alienbutt,"

Stoney finally said. "I've inputted the position of the gateway the best I remember into your onboard computer with all the star maps I have."

Alienbutt nodded and looked up at the sky. It was a couple of hours until sunset. "Thank you, you have done more for me than I could have hoped, Stoney, I now have a chance to get home."

"So what's your plan for your last night here with us?" Stoney asked, following Alienbutt's gaze to the top of one of the surrounding hills.

"I thought I'd walk up that hill there and watch the birds fly over. Care to join me?" Alienbutt replied with a smile as he set off walking. "It's a great sight to behold."

Stoney shrugged and set off after Alienbutt. "I fainted and stabbed your eye with a scalpel," he confessed. "I'm sorry, not good with the sight of blood."

"I know, I overheard one of the frogs talking yesterday," Alienbutt said, then changed the subject. "I used to watch the birds every evening with Wickede. He said it was good to share a bit of natural beauty with a friend, as it kept life in perspective."

Alienbutt sat on the top of the hill and watched as Stoney finally reached the top, his face red and his breathing heavy.

"What a stupid bloody idea. We could have seen your birds from half way up," Stoney said, throwing himself down next to Alienbutt, who passed him a bottle.

"Here, have a sip and stop moaning. Finally figured out the password on the replicator that Wickede put there to stop me drinking."

Stoney took a sip and smiled. "Whiskey?" he asked.

"Wickede said that when I got drunk I was no good for working the next day, so he put a password on the replicator to stop me drinking," Alienbutt said, smiling as the first of the giant birds flew over. "I always hoped if I watched often enough I would see two of the birds collide but they never do," Alienbutt said, taking the bottle back as the number of birds flying over increased as they headed for an evening down at the lake below.

"You do realise you have little chance of getting home, even if you somehow manage to get to the gateway. You could have a good life here. It's not that bad a place to live," Stoney said as the birds continued to fly over.

"I know, but I've got to try. Wickede is depending on me," Alienbutt said, draining the bottle. "Let's go back to the camp and I'll make you one of my special kebabs and we can drink some more."

# CHAPTER 8

## Killing in the Name of.

### INTERSTELLAR NEWS CHANNEL 9.
### NEWS FLASH.

The Coffee Houses and Federation senate today announced that the first crop of coffee containing the cure for its addiction has been harvested and it is expected that other production facilities are just days away. Senator Gralswige, flanked by members of the Coffee House board gave a special news interview in which he stated: "Despite the terrorist attacks upon the Coffee Houses and its staff by Ick backed extremists, the Coffee Houses have been working to bring the universe this cure. Today is a great day for the Federation and its people. With this cure and the war almost won we will soon enter a new era of peace and security. We prepare for a golden age of the Federation with coffee at its very heart."

The small shuttle landed in the docking bay of the secret base. Senator Gralswige was the final member of a secret order to arrive for the emergency meeting. The whole organisation had been rocked by the actions of just one man set on revenge. All of it was down to a failed assassination attempt. The target had escaped but it was thought his wife had been killed. Blackarachnia had so far killed a number of prominent members of the organisation's lower management, throwing parts of their operation into chaos, and had even started killing Galactic Senators who were bought and paid for. He was costing the Order a serious amount of money and trouble and that could not be tolerated. Now the fifteen-man ruling council had gathered to work out how to stop this extermination of their members, that ran not just the day to day business of coffee distribution but also the real business of controlling everything within the Federation.

As he walked down the ramp from his ship he was met in the docking bay by two men in black military uniforms and matching masks that hid their faces. These men were the organisation's assassins, the most highly trained killers outside of the mysterious Galactica assassins. With an afterthought he added Blackarachnia to that list of killers alongside those standing before him. His recent actions had thrown the most powerful organisation in the universe into a turmoil that no one would have foreseen or thought possible. As the doors to the lift closed he put his hand onto the scanner controls and then placed his eye up to the retinal scanner. Once his identity was confirmed the lift set off to the restricted lower levels where the other members waited. As always when the High Council of the Order met, security was tight, so even he only knew of the location when he was actually on his way there. As the lift came to a stop and the door opened Gralswige stepped into a large circular room. Around the edge of the room stood some thirty of the assassins, while seated at a large round table sat the council members. As he walked to his own seat he noticed the one next to his was empty. He paused for a second, realising that General Jee was not in attendance. Unsure of what that might mean, he continued to the table.

"The General has been delayed. It is another sign that this war may be taking a toll on him," said one of those sat at the table. Gralswige recognised the voice as that of the Lord High Coffee Baron, leader of the order. He always wore a cloak with the hood up so not even the members of this council knew his features or true identity.

"Are we to debate his future too then and his handling of the war?" asked Gralswige. As he spoke he saw movement from the corner of his eye. One of the assassins who had escorted him down had thrown a glowing orb into the air. As he turned to look, confused by his action, it exploded in searing white light, blinding all in the room.

Blackarachnia had infiltrated the assassins' chapter house and easily killed one of the assassins the same height and build as himself. He knew this chapter of assassins were the ceremonial guards of the High Council and would be present at any high council meeting. He had learnt of the secret meeting, so made his move just before the chosen assassins were to embark on the ship to it. An artificial voice box set to the dead assassin's exact vocal pitch completed the disguise, so he sounded just like the assassin he had replaced. The assassins rarely spoke unless it was necessary for a mission and would never remove their face masks when outside their chapter house, so his subterfuge would hold. He had spent two days watching his victim's every move using tiny nano cameras so he knew how to move and act to mimic the now dead assassin. He had watched the actions of the assassins with a detached manner, learning all he could, and felt nothing as he had driven the large knife into his back and up into the man's heart before dumping the body into the waste tubes leading to the incinerator. No one had realised the switch had been made and he had just sat back and allowed the Order to take him to where he needed to go. With the arrival of Gralswige and the news that the last member was not coming he acted.

Throwing the small orb up into the air he crouched down covering his face with his arm. Still the light was almost blinding, but by the time the initial explosion of light had vanished he had drawn two ornate hand guns from the holsters around his waist and opened fire to his left and right. Rolling forward towards the centre of the room he kept firing at the walls and the assassins who would still be stood there blinded, rubbing their eyes to try and recover their sight. Keeping his eyes closed to heighten his other senses he kept firing at where he heard movement. The guns that belonged to the assassin he had killed were totally silent as they discharged death to the dead man's comrades. The tools designed for their order's work turned upon them with a deadly result.

Finally opening his eyes he looked with still bleary vision but could make out figures moving and quickly opened fire again. Furiously blinking to clear the last of his blurred vision he began to count black-clad bodies even as he turned and opened fire at the people stumbling around at the table. Finally the guns were empty of bullets and he casually dropped them, pulling out fresh weapons from his belt as he sought new targets. He saw Gralswige stumbling away from the table, still blinded and not knowing where the threat to him would come from. Walking over to the Senator, Blackarachnia kicked him in the ribs sending him spinning across the floor. Shooting down a further two assassins as they stumbled towards him he walked over to the prone Gralswige and placed his boot on his chest to pin him down, then sent three bullets into his face. As Blackarachnia looked back to the table he felt something sting his arm. Looking over he saw the last of the assassins stood with weapon drawn. His face was hidden behind the black face mask, his gun pointed still towards the bounty hunter, awaiting any noise that would pin point him, as the assassin was still blind. Raising his gun he fired and the assassin flew backwards, blood spraying against the wall behind his head. Glancing at his upper arm he saw a graze where the bullet had skimmed past. Forgetting the wound he returned his attention to the table and the council members. Eight lay dead already; Gralswige was at his feet while the others stumbled around. Blackarachnia quickly shot down another three as he walked slowly towards the table. Pulling out a chair from the table he grabbed the fourth by the ankle. Dragging him out from beneath the table, he fired three shots into his back. Dropping the second set of guns he stood before the final council member. This one was still calmly seated, his face hidden by the large hood of his cloak.

"Blackarachnia, I presume?" he asked calmly, still not moving, his hands on the table before him. Blackarachnia reached up and removed the assassin's face mask he was wearing. With deliberate slowness he began to walk around the table to the last of the council members.

"Join with me Blackarachnia. Together we will end the war and you can rule the universe beside me."

Before the seated figure was a large shallow golden bowl filled with roasted coffee beans. Looking over to the far wall he saw an elaborate coffee bean grinder. He had noticed many of these grinders as he had worked his way through the Order's lower members, and now knew it was a sign of Order membership. Grabbing a handful of beans he yanked the Order's leader from his chair and dragged him over to the grinder, the hood of his cloak falling back to reveal his face.

"Blackarachnia, I can give you the master assassin that shot your wife. He was not following our orders when he shot her; you were both supposed to be taken alive," the order's leader pleaded, falling to his knees. Blackarachnia paused and looked at the terrified face looking back at him.

"Turn on the grinder," he ordered. The man nodded, tears now streaming down his face. As the machine came to life Blackarachnia threw the beans into the machine, listening to them as they were ground to a powder.

"They seemed like good quality beans," Blackarachnia observed, picking up the cup that had caught the ground beans. "Not your off the counter stuff I take it?"

"It's Kopi Luwak," answered the now terrified leader.

"The ones that that beetle shit out?" He threw the cup across the room in disgust. Then he stepped back and with a kick sent the ornate covering for the grinding blades clattering across the room, revealing the spinning disks used to grind the beans. Grabbing the hood of the cloak with one hand, he yanked the man up from his knees. With his other hand he grabbed the man's short grey hair. Bending down Blackarachnia looked into his terrified face, his fury evident and terrifying to behold.

"That is one disgusting drink, and I wouldn't ever trust you, and never would I join with any of you so-called leaders again. I will find your assassin and kill him in my own time. I don't need you for that. To be brutally honest I think you would say anything and sell out anyone to stay alive. You make me sick."

Blackarachnia began to force the man's head down towards the spinning blades. His pleading quickly turned to screams of pain as blood began to splatter over the grinder and up the wall behind. The blades suddenly stopped and Blackarachnia yanked back the Coffee House leader's head, half his lower face missing. A faint gurgling whimpering was all he could manage from his shattered face.

"Damn!" cursed Blackarachnia, looking at the tooth that had jammed the blades from spinning. The force of the blades suddenly split the tooth and the blades began to spin again. Blackarachnia's blood-splattered face split into a smile. "Let's try again shall we?" he said as again he pushed the head down for a final time.

General Jee walked into the secret chamber where the council meeting had been held. He had come down with just a handful of his most trusted men. The fewer people that saw what had occurred the better. He had not learned of the attack on the meeting until he had arrived, as no emergency call had been transmitted. The destruction up on the surface was extensive with most of the security detail dead from a chemical weapons attack. The many ships in the underground hangar belonging to the various Council members had been destroyed. The death count from this one attack was staggering; the Order had lost many of its top security personnel. That worried him far more than the fact that the whole High Council was amongst the dead. Their deaths saved him a job in the future, while highly trained security personnel would be hard to replace.

He walked over to where the body of the Lord High Coffee Baron lay by the ruined and gore-splattered coffee bean grinder. Turning over the body with his boot he saw that the face had been removed by the machine's blades. Turning from the sight he read the message on the wall above the grinder, written in blood and gore.

# YOU'RE NEXT JEE

Jee had no idea how Blackarachnia had found the location of this meeting. Not only that, he had got in and then killed the entire council before escaping. Jee was having a bad couple of days, as he had also been informed on his way to the meeting that Grommit had been rescued and his estates destroyed. He could feel his careful plans beginning to unravel as events were happening beyond his control. The Ick were proving harder to destroy than anyone thought, and he wasn't ready yet to take control openly of the inner systems. He looked down at the mutilated face of the leader of the Order of the Bean. Now he would never know what he looked like, he mused. He turned to the sergeant of arms he had brought down with him.

"Have the room purged as soon as we leave and order a video meeting of all surviving members. We have to reposition our forces quickly."

# CHAPTER 9

## The Secret Word.

INTERSTELLAR NEWS CHANNEL 9.
NEWS FLASH.

Reports are coming in that the leader of the Federal Senate, Senator Gralswige has been killed while visiting refugee camps along the Mushtaff System border. Early reports are saying the shuttle carrying the Senator and other high level personnel crashlanded after getting caught up in an unexpected solar storm. There are no reports of any survivors after rescue teams quickly located the wreckage. Tributes are already pouring in for the Senator who just days before announced that the cure for coffee addiction was to be rolled out to the universe.

General Jee, leader of the EDF and the new commander-in-chief of the Federal Navies said in a short statement: "Senator Gralswige worked tirelessly for the cause of freedom, a selfless person dedicated to the Federation and its people. I hope the cure for coffee addiction will be his lasting legacy to the universe and his sacrifice will never be forgotten."

The Fo'c'sle fleet returned to Ick space without further incident. The rescue attempt had been a great success; the Federation ships defending EV23 had all been destroyed without any losses. General Jee's estates now had been reduced to a pile of rubble after a prolonged bombardment once the away team had returned to Kali's ship. Then just for good measure and because they could they flew around the Coffee House owned planet destroying every building and energy source they picked up. Cyborgpirate had finally committed a devastating act of environmental vandalism by sending so many thermal charges at the north pole that he had melted the ice cap before starting to repeat the act at the south pole. Kali had ordered his first officer to sedate him so they could replace his personality chip that had shorted out, leaving him stuck in a homicidal killing rage with the planet becoming his selected target.

The fleet had returned straight to Dagnabbit, which was still being used as central command for the Ick fleet where Kali along with Killashandra, Grommit, Ponnfarr and the spy Whiff Morgan had been ordered to an immediate debriefing with Wickede and Snoodgrass.

Hydroponic sat staring at the scene before him, confused. There had been a battle here; well more accurately, there had been a pirate attack. Back when he first started out as a Bounty Hunter he had worked for a while hunting down the pirates who almost always turned out to be the Ji Hunters. One thing he had learnt from that time was if the Ji were beaten and unable to flee they would self-destruct their ships to avoid capture, so to see one of their ships floating lifeless was wrong. Hydroponic flicked a switch before him. "Nifty, get up here, we may have a problem."

Returning to the controls he set the long distance scanners to maximum sweep and then began to scan the wreckage of the ship before him. Nifty walked onto the bridge, her face covered in a white cream and sat down in the chair next to Hydroponic.

"Great, you wake me up in the middle of the night to show me a derelict ship. Have you been smoking in here?" she asked.

Not taking his eyes off the screen and the scan results Hydroponic answered; "Engines have been knocked out and there's substantial damage but the hull integrity is still whole, and no, I haven't been smoking."

"There's bits of baccy on the desk and you got the blowers on so don't try and lie. Now what's so important about this ship that you woke me up?"

Hydroponic finally turned to Nifty and jumped back in his chair, his eyes wide. "What the! Have you seen your face?" he asked looking puzzled at Nifty's face.

"Shut up and answer the question."

Hydroponic gave Nifty a final strange look and returned his attention to the screen. Spending time with Nifty aboard ship he had learnt a few valuable lessons. The main one was not to push observations about appearance or answer questions asked honestly, unless that answer was 'it looks great'. The second thing he learnt was a toilet seat had to be left down and life got easier the cleaner the bathroom was kept.

"It's a Ji pirate ship, you never ever see them drifting lifeless. They're either full of Ji trying to blow you up or exploding after you've beaten them. I need to teleport over there to check this out. What I need you to do is get me out at a moment's notice if it's a trap or I scream for help," Hydroponic said, still looking at the scan results. He then stood up and opened a chest next to his chair and pulled out his gun belt and an old assault rifle. "Beam me onto the flight deck. The hull integrity's intact there and keep an eye on the long range scanners, as it could be a trap."

Nifty stood up. "Give me five minutes to get dressed and take off my face mask."

"What!" Hydroponic said at Nifty who was already walking out. "Well, if it is a trap and the Ji attack, I'll ask them to wait while you get yourself ready."

"Thanks Hydro, and make me a cuppa while you're doing nothing. You know I need a cuppa when I first wake up." With that she was gone.

Hydroponic materialised on the bridge of the Ji ship. Emergency lighting lit the scene before him. The crew of the ship had been sliced up, arms and legs separated from bodies, razor sharp wounds evident everywhere he looked. Tapping a small camera by his ear he looked around.

"Nifty, are you getting this?"

A voice crackled into the earpiece. "Yes, get a close up on some of those injuries."

Hydroponic moved over to a decapitated body and knelt down before it. "Four parallel wounds, look like claw marks, Nifty."

"I know, this has to be Fluffy. He somehow got aboard and ripped through the crew. Looks like your Ji friends attacked the wrong ship."

"I thought you killed Fluffy on Blackarchnia's dreadnought when he attacked you?" Hydroponic asked, still looking around at the carnage.

"I thought I had, didn't get chance to double check though. Come on let's move on a bit," Nifty replied. Hydroponic stood up and looked to the captain's chair. The captain lay just before the chair, face down. His arm was almost severed and pinned to the arm of the chair by a long sliver of metal, his finger just short of the large red button. Walking over he turned over the body with his foot. The captain wheezed and coughed, blood coming from his mouth.

"Nifty we got a live one, prepare the med bay."

"No!" cried the captain. "Sit me in mi chair."

Carefully Hydroponic freed the arm and picked up the captain and sat him in the chair, the injured Ji struggling to avoid crying out in pain as he was moved. The captain sat and stared at Hydroponic and then smiled slightly in thanks.

"You need help before you bleed to death." Hydroponic said, covering the wound-severed limb with his hand to try and slow the blood loss. The Ji shook his head.

"You bin marked by Dream ma boy, I see it, I met 'im too when I wa a bairn. He told mi of ya and ow we would meet just afore I deed. You av to warn the Ji, the cat is real. They must start the hunt, I'll let yer know the secret word so ya get to see the Big Jee. Ya 'ave to warn tha Ji."

"What are you going on about?" Hydroponic asked, struggling to understand the captain.

"I git no time ta explain, Big Ji ill do that far ya when ya see im. Nar pin back ya lugs, ya need tha word and mi emblem." The captain indicated with a nod of his head a metal badge on his chest shaped like a shield. Hydroponic knelt before the dying Ji and unclipped the emblem from his shirt then listened as the captain whispered a single word.

"And that will stop me being blown up on sight?" Hydroponic asked. The captain closed his eyes and nodded.

"Aye, you take tha news back t' mi people, ma crew's names will go darn in istory, we are the first ta join the great pet hunt. Now you'd better bugger off afore I blow this tub up."

Hydroponic looked to the red button and the captain's hand that was now resting on it waiting to press it.

"Nifty, get me out of here," Hydroponic said, looking at the captain who nodded to him as he began to disappear.

Back aboard his own ship Hydroponic slumped into his

chair next to Nifty who sat watching the Ji vessel consumed by explosions.

"Well?" she asked.

"Seems your cat is known to the Ji, and he's not a friend. He's some sort of foreseen Nemesis or something."

"My cat?" asked Nifty "I should have left him behind on Sloppystool. Alienbutt always said he was trouble."

"Don't know about you but I'm getting sick to the back teeth of all this prophecy and soothsaying crap. Everywhere you turn there's someone shoving it down your throat."

"Well here's another mouthful for you Hydro; it's time to go see Wickede, the Book said I was to wait until we met your Ji there."

Hydroponic opened and shut his mouth a couple of times, trying to work out a response before standing up and storming back towards the quarters. "Damn it, it's your watch. I'm sick of all this crap."

Nifty waited until she heard him slam the door to his cabin and then leaned forward to flip the intercom.

"You left your cigars on the flight desk, Hydro."

She sat back and tried not to smile as he stormed back in and picked up the packet. When he had stormed back to his cabin she again leaned forward.

"You not need your lighter then?" she asked pleasantly. She didn't need the intercom to hear his scream.

The planet of Caprinae was isolated. It sat in the furthest reaches of the Outer Systems, far from the war that raged in the Ashia Minor belt. It was in an area of space that few ever visited as there was nothing to see when you got there. The reason for that was the most advanced planetary shielding and defence system known, or in this case not known. The people that lived on the planet lived a simple life, caring for their domestic herds of horned livestock, and took little notice of the outside universe unless someone actually took the trouble to seek them out. As no one knew of the planet apart from those that lived there, those people were often seeking ghosts. Even if they did find them, often the people of the planet would ignore their advances, but if they did decide to respond it would cost those people a vast amount.

The lady sat outside a simple domed building enjoying the warm summer evening. in her arms she held a small four-legged animal, absently scratching its head between the two small horns that were just starting to grow. The report she had received earlier was troubling. Someone was trying to seek out their planet. The Secret Order of the Bean had tried to do this not too long ago, but in a subtle way. As they were now all dead apart from General Jee, she knew it wasn't them. The Ick and their allies were too busy fighting a war they were losing to attempt such a foolish enterprise, and Snoodgrass was too smart to risk angering them. Yet a number of their contacts had disappeared, each one a step closer up the chain that would lead to them. In response she had dispatched a number of ships that morning to put an end to whoever was doing this. Her partner, known to the rest of the universe as the Galactica Assassin Death Ray was leading the mission, yet still she felt unease. The Galactica Assassins were feared by all, even those who used their services. Yet here was someone unknown acting in a hostile manner towards them, someone not afraid of the reaction of what the order would do to them. There was a new power growing in the universe, one that was so secret none knew of it. The only information they had so far was a single word, Fluffy.

# CHAPTER 10

## Heeter.

INTERSTELLAR NEWS CHANNEL 9.
NEWS FLASH.

News is coming in from planets that have received the new cured coffee that addiction levels are plummeting. Coffee consumption is now increasing per head of population as supply returns to pre-rationing levels. Business reports indicate productivity is increasing as it seems those using the new coffee are full of more energy. It is expected that coffee addiction will be wiped out within the year as the new coffee is supplied to more and more inner system planets.

Authorities are also reporting that the so called phenomenon of "Breakfast murders" has dropped by fifty per cent as people seem less edgy and volatile when they first wake up and are not feeling the need to cause violence to anyone that gets on their nerves.

Kali walked down the corridor of the ship, heading for the sleeping quarters of Ponnfarr. The mad pilot had served with her for many years, yet something about this mission had brought about a change in him. A warrior born he lived his life for the here and now, always making his presence known. He was a natural who threw himself into battle with a total disregard for his own safety, that made others follow his lead. During the height of the fighting in the Ashia Minor systems he had made suicidal charges, on many occasions turning the tide of battle and snatching victory from defeat. Yet this simple mission to formalise the change of sides of the Heeter system had almost seemed to scare him; he had withdrawn to his quarters for the two days of their flight so far.

When she reached his door she knocked and waited a moment. When there was no reply she entered. Ponnfarr sat cross-legged on his bed in his Fo'c'sle uniform, staring at a large ornate sword before him.

"Snoodgrass knows of my past, Commander, that's why I'm being sent with you," Ponnfarr said sadly. Kali shrugged and sat in the chair next to the bed. After a moment she leaned forward and put her hand around the hilt of the sword and picked it up.

"You were the most famous arena gladiator of your generation; a fair few of us knew who you were. We just respected the fact that you didn't want to trade on being that person when you joined us. Now you're a Fo'c'sle officer and we have a job to do. We need those Heeter shipyards, and while I dazzle the lecherous old king, you need to watch my back."

Ponnfarr sat thinking over her words and then he grinned. "You realise I will be challenged to single combat within hours of us getting there. We can find out our enemies by which gladiators challenge me."

"Let's hope you're not too old and rusty with that sword then, or your homecoming is going to be short," Kali said with a smile.

"Don't worry, the first challenge will be by some idiot with big muscles and no skill. I'll at least make it until dinner time," Ponnfarr said. "And no matter how rusty I get only the new champion would worry me."

Ponnfarr stood over the young gladiator's body. A long dagger in his hand was reversed so it pointed back along the length of his forearm. It dripped blood onto the polished floor of the royal court. He stood in his Fo'c'sle uniform, the large sword strapped across his back unused. Kali was impressed; the gladiator had challenged Ponnfarr as soon as they had been introduced to the court. A nod from the old king and the people had drawn back to give the two room to fight. The gladiator dwarfed the Fo'c'sle fighter, he was bare-chested and full of muscles, swinging a great sword with ease. Ponnfarr had taken a step forward, smiling as he drew a dagger from his belt. Seconds later the gladiator was dead, his throat sliced so deep his head was almost removed. For a while the crowd seem stunned, then all began to cheer and chant Ponnfarr's name. After a minute of the chanting the king stood up and order was restored.

"Well, my old champion, it seems you still know how to knife fight," the old king said with a grin.

Ponnfarr sheathed his dagger and bowed to the King. "The Lord Sthrom needs to train his puppies better. May I introduce to you my companion, Commander Kali of the Fo'c'sle, emissary to the Ick Empire?"

Kali stepped forward and bowed her head towards the King who sat looking her up and down.

"If I was twenty years younger I would make you my queen.

Come sit by me." The King indicated a chair beside him. Kali smiled and walked forward, Ponnfarr a few steps behind her. As she took the seat she smiled as she replied to the King.

"It's a good job you are not twenty years younger then. You already have three queens and I don't play well with others."

The King grinned. "Snoodgrass chose well in sending you. He knows my weakness for feisty women." He reached over and laid his hand onto Kali's leg.

"He did indeed," replied Kali coldly. "The other two choices would have gutted you already for putting your hand on them. I tend to give a warning first and you just got it." She smiled sweetly at the King.

The King looked into Kali's face and saw she wasn't joking and removed his hand, forcing a laugh. Lowering his voice so none of the court could hear, he whispered:

"We will wait for the next challenge to Ponnfarr and then we will all retire to a more private room to discuss matters. Snoodgrass did his homework well in sending you. You're a natural at Heeter court niceties and know how to put an old king in his place. As long as Ponnfarr hasn't grown rusty, you both should live long enough to sort out our switch in sides."

From the back of the hall came a disturbance. As the crowd parted, Kali saw a man of middle years striding down the hall, flanked by at least ten of the bare-chested gladiators. All were heavily muscled and had large swords strapped across their backs.

"Here comes the next challenge," the King chuckled, as he watched the display of the new arrivals. Halfway down the hall the man stopped, his gladiators spread out behind him. All in the hall fell silent.

"Lord Malward, how nice of you to attend my court. We have noted your absence," the King said, loud enough for all to hear, and all could tell he sounded anything but pleased.

"My King, I am here to arrest the enemy of the Federation sitting by your side," The newcomer announced. Ponnfarr took a step forward, placing himself in front of Kali. Slowly drawing his sword he held it with the tip touching the floor before him.

"It seems you must meet the challenge of her champion first. These traditions are a pain but must be observed." The King held out his hands in mock sorrow at the events and Ponnfarr's challenge. Lord Malward's eyes blazed and with a nod of his head one of the gladiators stepped forward.

"Then it is a formality. Tallfarr champion of the arena will fight on my behalf, undefeated in three hundred battles and undisputed Lord of the Arena."

The King leaned over to Kali, sounding a little worried. "I wasn't expecting the big guns just yet; we may have a problem."

Kali looked at the King. "What are Ponnfarr's chances against this Tallfarr?"

The King shrugged. "Fifteen years ago in his prime, pretty good. Now, I would say not quite so good to no chance at all. Tallfarr is unstoppable."

Kali looked down toward Ponnfarr who had turned and stood facing her. He gave her a half smile before mouthing a single word: "Shit."

"What can you do to stop this?" Kali asked.

"Nothing, it is between the Lord Malward and yourself. No one else can interfere. Only the two of you and your champions may act," the king replied.

Kali smiled. "Well, why didn't you say that?" In one fluid movement Kali stood and drew her handgun. Before anyone could react she put a hole in the head of Lord Malward and then another into the gladiator Tallfarr's head. In the stunned silence she shouted out to the hall: "If my champion is to fight any more today then it will be against someone fitting of his skill and history. He will not give anyone else a name by killing them himself. Anyone have a problem with that?"

Silence greeted her announcement, then she heard the King begin to laugh. "I think you have the agreement of my court. Let us all retire to my private rooms and have some food."

Kali glanced down at Ponnfarr, who stood grinning up at her. "You're a natural at Heeter politics. I think the King will want this deal signed and you off planet before you end up ruling. Hell, you just replaced the third most powerful man on the planet and we've only been here an hour."

Kali looked confused until a woman of stunning looks stepped towards her and smiled. "Matters of honour are settled by our gladiators because if the nobles are killed then the winner takes over their position and lands, leaving their families with nothing. Although your actions were within the rules you have broken uncounted guides to court protocol, my Lady Malward." She turned to Ponnfarr and smiled. "Hello Ponnfarr, long time no see."

"Princess," Ponnfarr replied, blushing, then he remembered to bow. "You look good, I mean well."

The Princess smiled at Ponnfarr's discomfort before turning and following the King. Kali turned back to Ponnfarr, looking questioningly at him.

"The Princess, she is the second most powerful person on the planet," Ponnfarr stammered.

"Why do I suspect a history between you two?" Kali looked past Ponnfarr to where Malward's surviving gladiators had advanced and now knelt before her, their swords lain on the floor before them. "What the hell is this?" she asked.

Ponnfarr turned around and looked down at them. "They are yours to command, as are all Malward's people. You own everything that was his. You're rich enough to retire and spend the rest of your life being an extravagant noble."

"I now understand why you're so strange. You come from a planet full of nutters," Kali said in disbelief as she turned to follow the King, ignoring the gladiators.

Ponnfarr looked at the confused gladiators and shrugged. "Don't worry, she's an off-worlder so a little strange. Send word about your new mistress and await her orders."

Kali walked into the King's private audience rooms to see the King receiving an injection from a medical droid. She paused at the door but the King beckoned her forward.

"Come in Commander, we are just about done," he said brightly. Kali looked around the room. The Princess and half a dozen others were present.

"Are you unwell, your Majesty?" she asked diplomatically.

"I'm dying, Commander," he stated with a smile. "If not for these drugs and twice daily blood transfusions, then the poison would have already killed me." The King indicated everyone should sit and then continued. "Heeter has the largest independent shipyards in the Federation. It seems the Federation want to do a take-over, and that means it's the Coffee Houses that want them. I was poisoned about a month ago by a Coffee House assassin, so it's been decided that in the interests of staying independent we should join with the Ick."

"You need our forces to defend your planets then," Kali replied, sitting back in her seat.

"No, our defences are more than adequate to defend from any outside attack. What I need is Ponnfarr to defend my daughter the Princess from internal attacks upon her."

Kali sat back up, shocked. She looked over at the Princess, who wasn't doing a good job of hiding her fury at the King's words. From behind her she heard Ponnfarr gasp. The King held up his hand to prevent anyone speaking so he could continue.

"Ponnfarr will marry my daughter and be her consort, defending her from those who would try to replace her when I die. In return the Ick get to use our shipyards."

The Princess jumped to her feet in fury. "You never said this was your plan in inviting them here, and you expect me to marry him? He's old," she complained, pointing a hand shaking with fury at Ponnfarr.

From behind her Kali heard Ponnfarr mumble. "This has got to be a joke. Please refuse," he pleaded.

Kali looked at the Princess and then back at the King. Finally she smiled. "You have a deal. So, when do we announce the happy event?"

# CHAPTER 11

## The King's Plan.

INTERSTELLAR NEWS CHANNEL 9.
NEWS FLASH

In sports news the Hardstool F.A. today announced that the rebuilding work on the International sports arena will continue despite being five billion over budget and two years past the completion date. A spokesman for the supporters' trust, New Lothian Pride claims the Hardstool F.A. could not organise a piss-up in a brewery. The original stadium was destroyed by an unknown anti-football group to cover the theft of the football relic the Wembley goal post. To date no arrests have been made over the act of sports terrorism and the whereabouts of the goalpost is still unknown.

Ponnfarr sat staring over at the Princess, it had been decided that they needed to spend time getting to know each other. The Princess had raged for hours after her father and Kali had struck the deal, until finally the King had ordered the two escorted to the room, as he was getting a headache. Since the door had been shut and bolted from the outside the Princess had become quiet, but Ponnfarr was not fooled. He knew she was even more dangerous now than when she had been screaming.

Picking up a piece of fruit from a plate beside him, he decided it was time to strike up conversation.

"So how's your day been?" He knew it was a stupid thing to say as he said it. The Princess's head snapped around and her eyes bore into him.

"What?" she screamed. He watched as she fought a losing battle to control herself. "Let me see, where should I begin?" She took a step towards him and Ponnfarr found himself trying to push himself through the heavy chair.

"Well, it started quite well. We had a little bloodshed and your friend really gave the court gossips loads to mull over. Then my father sold me off in some business deal, so I have to marry some sad old gladiator."

"I'm not old," Ponnfarr said defensively.

"Don't interrupt me!" she screamed. Again she paused as she worked to gain control of herself. Finally she continued in a calm voice; "I am to be the next Queen. I am trained in armed combat as well as court politics. Do I look like I need someone to look after me?" She looked down at Ponnfarr in contempt. "Especially from the likes of you."

Ponnfarr slowly stood up, holding the Princess's gaze, his eyes blazing. He saw doubt in her eyes for an instant, but she held her ground.

"You look like someone who always got their own way

by screaming and stamping her feet. I fear your father forgot to punish you often enough when you were..." He paused, considering his options. "I was going to say a child, but you still are. The worst spoilt child I've ever met."

The Princess's arm flew forward and Ponnfarr swayed to his left as a dagger flew past his head. "If you ever touch me I will remove your hand," she warned him.

Ponnfarr smiled. "If I ever touch you I will remove my own hand, Princess." Ponnfarr swayed to his right this time as another dagger was thrown. "And if you throw another dagger, princess or not, I'll knock you off your feet."

Ponnfarr ducked as two throwing stars flew through the space where his head had been.

"Those were not daggers, old man. I take poorly to threats but I would hate for you to think I don't listen," the Princess said, smiling sweetly. "Glad to see your reactions are not too old and rusty."

Ponnfarr took a deep breath as he tried to keep control of his temper. He was trapped in this situation; Kali's agreement had seen to that, but he couldn't spend the rest of his life dodging daggers.

"Listen, Princess, the last thing I want to do is marry you. Tales of your tantrums are used in the Outer Systems to terrify young men into behaving," Ponnfarr snarled as he prepared himself to speak his mind. He was so intent on speaking his mind that he didn't hear the noise coming from outside the room. "You have to be the most spoilt person I've ever met." The Princess went to open her mouth, but Ponnfarr held up his hand to indicate silence.

"Don't speak, it's my turn now, and after listening to you for so long I deserve to be heard." The Princess moved to her left, putting a large table between herself and Ponnfarr. "I am a soldier and will do as ordered, but this has to be the worst mission I have ever been given."

The Princess crouched down behind the table as the door exploded inwards. When she stood back up she was holding an assault rifle that she aimed at the doorway, so as the first battle droid walked through she opened fire, blowing off its head and sending it back through the door crashing into those that followed it.

Ponnfarr stood unmoving as the door exploded inwards. He registered the Princess ducking behind the table and felt the large wooden splinter that pierced his arm. He turned to see the first battle droid lose its head and slowly he drew his handgun. Watching the doorway he turned a dial on the side of the gun and aimed, firing a single round. The area outside the room exploded into flame.

"Incendiary shells?" the Princess observed with a grin. "Nice."

Ponnfarr shrugged his shoulders. "Standard issue secondary shells. Now stop changing the subject, this isn't over, Princess. I've still got a lot to say."

The Princess looked at him in disbelief. "You do realise the palace is under attack?"

"A few Federation battle droids is hardly an attack, Princess," he replied. A large explosion ripped through the palace, knocking both of them off their feet as part of the roof collapsed. As the dust began to settle, Ponnfarr looked through the hole in the roof, to see Federation ground attack ships flying over.

"I think those ships do hint we may be under attack though. I need to get you to safety, Princess; it appears the palace could be under attack."

The Princess stood and aimed the assault rifle towards the doorway. "As we are not married yet I will do as I please, and I've decided to counter-attack." With that she set off and walked through the ruined doorway. Almost immediately more battle droids came into view down the corridor. Calmly the Princess opened fire and the droids were cut down. Ponnfarr cursed and set off after her.

"Princess, we need to get to where your loyal troops are. You can't counter-attack all by yourself. You only do that when you have back up."

"But I'm not alone. I've got my future protector with me, and you counter-attacked all by yourself many times on the Ashia minor front." The princess threw Ponnfarr a smile. "You think I haven't heard of your exploits many times from my father? So don't give me that 'get reinforcements' crap." She opened fire as more battle droids appeared. "What's wrong? You got gun envy? Is my gun bigger than yours?"

Ponnfarr cursed and turned the dial on his handgun again before aiming it down the hallway.

"Size isn't important. I suggest you duck." With that he fired and the other end of the corridor disappeared in an explosion that brought down the ceiling.

The Princess had crouched down as Ponnfarr had suggested and as the dust cleared she looked up to the still-standing Fo'c'sle pilot and grinned.

"You've got to get me one of those guns," she said in awe.

"Who's got gun envy now?" he replied, grinning back, then both realised they were on the verge of being nice to each other and looked away, falling into silence. Finally the Princess spoke; "The throne room then. As you've just demolished the most direct route, we will have to go the long way round."

Kali strode across the throne room as all around the palace guards ran to defensive positions as the attack upon the palace began. Somehow Federation battle droids had got within the walls and taken those guards upon the wall by surprise. Those droids were being quickly found and dispatched, but now new waves of attackers were approaching. The king stood upon the dais, holding onto the arm of the throne as his aides quickly strapped on his regal body armour. In his youth he would have looked impressive, but now he looked like an old man wrapped in armour three times too large for him. He saw Kali and smiled at her.

"Would you believe this used to be fit perfectly? Either it's stretched or I've grown old," the King said brightly, his eyes shining with excitement at the prospect of a fight.

"My dreadnought will be in the air and here within minutes, and troops loyal to your Majesty are moving up to engage the rear of the forces attacking," Kali said with a slight smile. "And you still look impressive in your armour," she lied.

The King smiled. "No I don't. I'm an old man, but I will die in my armour."

"You think the battle lost already?" Kali said, surprised by the King's statement.

"Long range sensors have picked up a Federation fleet that has just jumped out of light speed. We are betrayed, and our outer defences are even now allowing the Federation through. There's heavy fighting in all our military bases as troops loyal to me are being attacked by traitors, backed up by Federation attack droids."

"Your orders then?" asked Kali, realising that Heeter was lost, and with it also their shipyards.

The King smiled as a large sword was strapped across his back. "I made plans. The shipyards will not be captured intact; thermal devices will mean the Federation have to rebuild before they can use them, and all computers will be wiped of technical data. Our men will stand to the last while you get my daughter aboard your ship and get out of here. All loyal fleet that are able will leave with you and take up her cause in exile."

Kali stepped forward, a look of fury on her face. "So this was your plan all along. You needed us to save your daughter's life when you were overthrown. You dangled the shipyards in front of us to ensure we would come."

The King met Kali's gaze and held it.

"I knew this day would come the minute I was poisoned. The Heeter nobles would never accept the Princess as their ruler. My sons were killed in the battle of Dagnabbit, maybe by one of your squadron; I know they fought in that battle. It was only a matter of time before I was overthrown, but I will not lose my daughter too. She's all I have left," the King replied sadly, the pain of his loss evident for Kari to see. More explosions rocked the palace as Kali stepped back. She held the King's gaze a moment longer, then nodded. She raised her wrist to speak into her com-link.

"Ponnfarr, get yourself to the throne room now, and ensure the Princess is by your side and kept safe."

"Almost there, Commander. The Princess is with me but insists on shooting every droid we come across," responded Ponnfarr's voice over the com-link.

"I don't care if you have to throw her over your shoulder and carry her, get her here now," demanded Kali. She turned as she sensed someone approaching her from behind. The head of the Malward gladiators stood there and bowed. He was covered in blood, and a rough bandage was tied round his arm.

"My lady, the Malward forces stand awaiting orders. The gladiators here have fought beside the King's men, but the bulk of our men await your word before joining battle."

Kali looked back to the King. "What the hell is he on about? Why do they wait for my orders?"

"The Malward forces are yours to command. You became the lady Malward when you killed the last lord," the King said, as he shrugged his shoulders. "The men are yours by law and await orders to join the battle, and need to know which side to join."

"Bloody stupid Heeter laws." She turned back to the gladiator, knowing she was issuing a death sentence. "You fight for your King until the end. May it bring you glory."

The gladiator grinned up at her. "Glory and more honour than we hoped while with the old lord, my lady. We serve our King, and gladly prepare to bleed for him."

There was a commotion at the end of the hall, a squealing cutting through the noise of the hall. Silence fell as everyone turned to see Ponnfarr walk in with the Princess over his shoulder, kicking and screaming. He quickly walked up to the dais and unceremoniously dumped the Princess onto the floor.

"She refused to leave the defensive perimeter. You did say to get her here fast," Ponnfarr explained defensively. Kali looked at him and noticed four large scratch marks down his face.

"The Princess?" she asked. Before he could reply, the Princess sprang to her feet and punched Ponnfarr full in the face, making him stagger backwards.

"Damn right the Princess, and that time I couldn't get a proper swing at the animal, so had to settle for a scratch. I want him arrested for laying hands on me," she demanded of her father.

"I think not, daughter. He was following my direct order," said the King. "Now I know you wanted a big wedding, but there isn't time. So before those here, I give you in marriage to Ponnfarr. He is to protect you and all the rest of that stuff, blah-de blah." The King looked at Ponnfarr. "Accept my daughter by command of your King and protect her with your life, blah-de-blah. You're now married."

One of the King's retainers stepped forward and handed

the shocked Ponnfarr a scroll. The King grinned at him. "You are named Prince of Heeter and protector of the royal house. You may kiss your bride."

Ponnfarr looked at the Princess, who stared back with hatred in her eyes.

"Try it and I'll gut you," she hissed at him.

"Maybe I'll wait until we know each other a little better, your Majesty," Ponnfarr answered, still in shock. "And only if she asks me nicely."

The King handed a scroll to Kali. "It's all legal and the paperwork signed, Commander." He stepped forward towards his daughter and quietly said to her; "It's for the best, my daughter. You need a strong man by your side in the days to come." Before she could respond he stepped back and turned back to Kali. "Are you ready, Commander?"

Kali nodded and reached over, placing a small bracelet onto the shocked Princess's wrist. Then she raised her arm.

"Three to beam up, then get us out of here before the Federation fleet turns up."

The King stood and watched as his daughter disappeared, then holding onto the arm of his throne, turned to his commanders.

"Order the shipyards fired and then we prepare to launch a counter–attack. We go out taking the fight to the traitors." A great cheer greeted his words and he took advantage of it to turn to his aide. "Take this bloody sword off my back; the weight is killing me. There's no way I can walk with it on."

He turned back to those assembled. "Order all ships that are able, to retreat to Ick lines and meet up with the Princess, ready to start a counter-offensive with her and her new husband, the Prince Ponnfarr. The traitors may have won this battle, but the future Queen will win the war, and our last stand will echo down into the future to show we fell with honour."

Minutes later the first of the Federation fleet arrived in orbit and launched a thermal missile strike that vaporised the palace and all key locations of the King's force, abruptly ending their final stand.

# CHAPTER 12

## Fluffy Hunt.

### INTERSTELLAR NEWS CHANNEL 9.
### NEWS FLASH.

News is coming in from the Heeter system of a rebellion led by the King's daughter. Fierce fighting has raged on the planet and only the arrival of a Federal fleet prevented the planet falling to the Princess and her forces. It is believed the Princess has escaped with a handful of rebels after using thermal weapons to destroy the royal palace and a number of military targets. The King and many of his court were killed during the attempted uprising. General Jee has assumed control of the planet until the succession to the throne can be verified. Teams of engineers are working to repair large-scale damage caused to the shipyards during the uprising. The Heeter shipyards were the largest production site in the Inner Systems, producing forty per cent of the merchant fleets.

Mr Fluffy had learnt much from his battle with Nifty. The battle suit had been found wanting and had been too easily damaged. He had worked since then on improving it, using first the equipment delivered by the Federation assassin, and then from a number of secret science laboratories scattered around the Federation, that he had secretly taken over. Each laboratory had been infiltrated and then the staff implanted with either his mind control chips or nano-probes to ensure their obedience. His battle suit was now much improved, being more manoeuvrable and equipped with weaponry and shielding that made it safe from every conceivable attack. With the suit ready he had decided that it would need field testing, as he could not afford another setback as his planning for universal domination continued. A need within himself drove him on, telling him that he needed to be ready for the real battle that would come after he took over the universe. He would have to face his true enemies and any weakness then would lead to failure. He had already attacked a training base for E.D.F. Special forces and had run amok, killing everyone there. It had proved to be a poor test and far too easy, but by chance he had discovered something far better to test his suit. For the last month he had begun to bait a new trap, hunting down and killing agents that worked for the Galactica assassins. He knew that they would eventually send out agents to find out who was threatening their order's security.

From the last agent he had killed, he had gained the information he needed to know of the next agent up the chain. Also he knew that when he arrived to kill the next agent their assassins would be waiting for him. This would be a true field test of his battle suit. He would face the ultimate hunters in the universe at a place of their choosing, a remote little trading post known as Molvan Moon.

As his ship approached the small moon that orbited a large

gas planet that was close to the Ji border, his sensors picked up traces of a cloaked ship. He had refined and improved the sensor array of the ship so that nothing could escape detection. The ship was invisible to usual sensor sweeps, but the designers of the cloaking device had failed to anticipate one small detail; the crew would flush the toilet. The ship had been sitting in orbit for just over a day, and so his sensors picked up tiny traces of frozen humanoid waste and pine-scented chemicals floating close to the ship. Purring in delight Mr Fluffy took his ship into orbit close to where the cloaked ship was hidden, then without warning fired a spread of torpedoes that destroyed the ship before they could react to his sudden attack. He watched the explosions as they ripped through the invisible ship, revealing it as the power supply to the cloaking device failed. Then, still purring, he teleported down to the trading post, ready to face the now alerted assassins.

Death Ray sat in the small office of their agent, finishing a cup of coffee. Even had she not been human then, the still addictive effects of the illegally grown bean would not have bothered her. The Galactica had discovered the secret cure many years before and had recently pointed the Ick in the right direction. The trading post was a small nondescript outpost like many others dotted around in the less travelled areas. A giant atmospheric dome covered the trading post, giving the air a damp fusty smell. The Galactica were taking no chances with whoever was trying to find them, as their agent network had been infiltrated further than at any time in the order's history. Ten fully trained assassins had been dispatched with her. Even when they had carried out the attempted assassination of Wickede, she had only led a team of four assassins, with the rest of their numbers made up by trusted mercenaries. This threat was being taken very seriously, and they intended to end it here.

When their ship informed them of the arrival of an unmarked ship, Death Ray sent out the assassins to take up position; not that they would need her to tell them what to do. Each one was an expert at their craft and could work alone or in a team. They would discover and kill whoever was behind the attempts to infiltrate them, and then destroy everyone connected with them. Finishing her drink, she stood ready to take up position, when their agent who was monitoring the approaching ship, gasped.

"What is it?" Death Ray asked, turning to look at him.

"It's the new arrival. It's just destroyed your ship even though it was still cloaked." He looked up as an alarm sounded within the room. "My Lady, someone has teleported into the dome."

Death Ray walked to the door. "Stop panicking, you are a professional. Lock down this room. I want you watching all the post's cameras." As soon as she was through the door it shut behind her and she heard the heavy magnetic locks thud into place. Already she heard gunfire and explosions off to her left, and began to move that way. The destruction of her ship was a shock, but she put it aside as she began to hunt, concentrating on the messages coming over the com-link from her fellow assassins. Their prey had materialised in the central square and began killing locals there.

Mr Fluffy materialised in the centre of the trading post, a large open area with streets leading off like the spokes of a wheel. Around him three or four shocked people stood, slowly backing away from him. A quick glance showed they were unarmed and residents of the trading post. Being of no use to him Mr Fluffy casually opened fire, cutting them down. Within seconds the first assassin opened fire at him, an explosive dart detonating as it hit the shielding surrounding his battle suit. This was followed almost instantly by an electro-blast that sent sparks flying as it too hit the shield, as the assassin changed rounds, testing the shielding. Mr Fluffy looked over to where the shots had come from, and using infra-red, picked out the assassin's hiding place. He was about three buildings back from those that faced the central square of the trading post. Zooming in on the assassin, using the battle suit's visual sensors, Mr Fluffy began to purr as he saw the assassin taking aim again through a partially open window. In one fluid movement Mr Fluffy raised his arm and fired. The round from his arm-mounted gun punched a hole through the wall of the building before lifting the assassin off his feet, his chest exploding from the impact. Taking just two steps he came under more fire, this time from his right as an assassin fired multiple rounds; again they hit the shielding and ricocheted away. As Mr Fluffy turned to face the new attack, a second assassin fired an incendiary grenade that engulfed him in a giant fireball. Ignoring the second attack, he focused on the first attacker as they moved to a new position. Raising his arm again a small panel slid back as a small three-inch missile slid out. Firing instantly, it shot down the street and around the corner, homing in on the fleeing assassin. Sensing something approaching him the assassin dropped to the floor hoping to dodge, but the missile changed direction to strike him in the back before exploding. Spinning around, Mr Fluffy searched for the other assassin. Infra-red showed nothing, so he began flicking through other sensors. Within seconds he discovered his hiding spot, using an object density scan to beat her cloaking device. He purred in delight that this new scan he had invented worked, and raising his other arm, sent a hail of bullets that destroyed the wall she was hiding behind, ripping the assassin to shreds. He would have to continue working on the object density scan to increase its range, he decided.

Death Ray came to a stop. Stepping close to the wall, she crouched down. In less than a minute the three assassins who had been watching the central courtyard had been killed. She knew each of them and was shocked at the speed of their deaths. Their prey was far more skilled than anyone they had ever faced before. Pressing a button on her belt, she shimmered and disappeared from normal sight. Lifting her arm she flipped back a cover on her wrist and pressed other buttons that would block out any sign of body heat. Finally happy that all defensive precautions had been carried out, she pressed a final button, sending a "kill on sight" order to the remaining assassins. Their target was too dangerous to take any more chances with. Replacing her gun in its holster she then moved forward. Already she knew the other assassins would have taken the same precautions as she had. She was already starting to suspect that the role of hunter and prey had been reversed.

Mr Fluffy stood still in the centre of the square and began to scan the entire trading post. Heat signs from basements revealed the local residents had quickly found hiding places as the shooting had begun. One building at the far end was shielded from his attempts to scan it, so he knew that would be the place where the Galactica agent would be. Of the assassins he could find no trace with any of his scans. They had disappeared and must now be using their cloaking devices; the hunt was now on in earnest. He began to walk towards the agents'building. With no traces showing of the assassins for him to home in on, he would make the assassins come for him.

The assassin clung to the wall unmoving as the robotic form of his prey walked down the street beneath him. Totally invisible, his form blended in without the slightest trace of his presence. On the wall opposite was a second assassin also hidden in the same manner, while a third lay on the floor just in front of them. As their prey walked beneath them they sprang, laser swords at the ready to slice though his metallic armour. In mid fall their prey sensed them and raised his arms, laser shields appearing on each arm deflecting their strikes. The assassin on the floor leapt forward, his sword thrust towards the chest area to deliver a killing blow. The assassin watched in shock as their victim easily deflected the attack of the other two assassins, then leapt with unbelievable speed and dexterity over him to avoid his own attack. Twisting in mid-air, the unknown target came down clear of the three and spun to face them. All three took up a fighting stance ready to attack again, each of them confident with their weapon. When their opponent raised his arm and fired at them, they easily deflected the bullets with their swords, then began to edge forward ready to launch a second co-ordinated attack. Their prey began to purr loudly. Within seconds the noise rose to a painful level and the buildings' walls began to shake with the vibrations of the noise, the effects of the noise amplified by the narrow enclosed street. The assassins struggled to stay on their feet, with blood beginning to stream from their noses and ears. All the while, the sonic vibrations continued to increase. Dropping his sword, the centre assassin fell to his knees as pain racked his body. He was vaguely aware that his companions had also fallen. He knew he was going to die, even before their intended prey walked forward and casually picked up his dropped sword. He didn't notice that the purring had stopped as he watched his own sword swing forward to remove his head.

The Galactica agent watched the cameras in disbelief as the attacker coolly picked up the kneeling assassin's sword and casually decapitated him before doing the same to the other two. Six of the assassins had been easily dispatched by this robotic attacker with ease and still it approached him. On the verge of panic he began to grab essential items and stuff them into a bag.

Death Ray stood with the remaining assassins. They had watched the latest attempt on their target through small screens on their gauntlets. They stood on the flat roof of a building off to the left of the latest encounter.

"Opinions?" Death Ray asked of the others, glad that her voice sounded calm.

"We are overmatched. This opponent is shielded against our firearms and has reflexes even faster than our own. We need more information on what we face and the weapons he has. We should retreat and face him again with support so we can learn more and maybe find a weakness," replied one. The others murmured agreement.

"I agree. We order the agent to launch his defence missiles to distract the ship in orbit, then we make our escape in the agent's shuttle."

A large crash behind them caused all four to spin, weapons drawn. Somehow their opponent had found them and now stood on the far side of the roof. The four assassins spread out cautiously, watching for any hint of movement from their opponent.

"Are you leaving so soon? The game has only just begun," he asked.

"I just remembered I have a prior engagement," replied Death Ray, noticing the large cracks in the roof where their opponent had landed. "We'll be right back, so who do we ask for?"

A soft purring came from the metallic figure. "Funny, you humans always try humour when scared. I am Mr Fluffy, and soon I will be known by everyone."

Death Ray smiled and then all four assassins open fire, not aiming at Mr Fluffy but at the floor at his feet, Mr Fluffy raised his arms to return fire just as the roof collapsed and he disappeared. Death Ray dived to her right but felt a sting on her arm, the assassin to her left was less fortunate and was lifted back and over the side of the roof as bullets ripped through his chest. Rolling to her feet Death Ray threw a thermal grenade through the hole in the roof and then jumped as a fireball exploded upwards and the building shook before collapsing in on itself.

Hitting the floor hard Death Ray gasped as the wound on her arm sent out waves of pain, but she staggered to her feet and ran for their agent's office, the remaining two assassins a step behind. By the time they reached the office the agent stood with the door open.

"Quickly, your opponent has just climbed out of the wreckage of the building and is heading this way," he said in a panicked voice.

Death Ray cursed. "Can nothing stop that thing?" She looked back to where a cloud of smoke still rose. "We need your emergency shuttle."

The agent ushered the assassins inside and closed the door. "All information has been transferred to the shuttle and the computers wiped, my Lady. The missile silos will give a covering fire when we launch. The entrance to the tunnel is behind that unit," he said, indicating a large metal unit against the wall. One of the assassins stepped forward and slid the unit to one side, revealing a pair of double doors. Pressing a button, the doors slid open to reveal a lift.

"It is a turbo lift; it will have us in the hangar within minutes. Everything is ready for our escape."

Death Ray turned to the agent and withdrew her pistol. "Your services are no longer needed." With that she shot the unfortunate man and without a backward glance entered the lift.

Mr Fluffy climbed out of the rubble. His vision sensors were flickering and a weapons malfunction on his right arm would mean it was useless until he could repair it. The heat of the thermal grenade had melted the metal structure of the building within seconds, causing its collapse, but his battle suit had withstood it with acceptable damage. Finally the sensor array fully rebooted and Mr Fluffy set off after the fleeing assassins. As he reached the building of the Galactica agent, he received a message that his ship was under attack from missiles fired from the planet, and that a shuttle had launched. He was about to order himself beamed aboard the ship when the agent's building in front of him exploded. The blast picked up Mr Fluffy and he was thrown backwards to smash through a building behind him. The force of the explosion had flattened all buildings within fifty feet, and as Mr Fluffy got back to his feet he heard a large cracking noise. Looking up he saw the dome of the trading outpost's environmental bubble covered in large cracks. Seconds later the dome gave way and the contents of the bubble were blown out to the non-atmosphere of the small moon.

Mr Fluffy was beamed aboard his ship minutes later, but the assassins had escaped. His battle suit had worked well and not even the freezing cold of the moon's surface had affected its operation. The Galactica assassins had given it a field test more rigorous than expected, but he was still operational. He had easily defeated a team of ten of the deadliest killers in the universe. Nothing now could stand against him as he continued to plan his rise to rule the universe, yet a voice within his head warned him not to underestimate the Alienbutt. Dismissing such thoughts, he opened the hatch on the battle suit and nimbly jumped out. Sitting down he began to wash himself, as a member of the ship's crew placed a bowl of milk in front of him and began to wind up a small clockwork mouse. Purring in excitement, Mr Fluffy waited to pounce as the mouse was placed on the floor.

Ponnfarr sat silently in the meeting hall. His new wife stood ready to explode in fury. She had ordered a meeting with the commanders of the Heeter fleet that had escaped as the Federation-backed traitors had taken over their home system. After outlining her plans for the fleet's operation, the fleet Admiral had politely just informed her that she would act only as a figurehead for her people and would have no part in the planning of the upcoming offensive. Ponnfarr was becoming quite impressed at the way she was learning to control her temper since their escape, but this meeting was a true test for her.

The new Queen took a deep breath. "Are you telling me you are refusing to follow my royal orders, Admiral?"

The Admiral smiled at her. He was now head of the Heeter forces and while not a total idiot, he still held the rank because of a noble family upbringing rather than skill. This lack of real skill and experience combined with a sexist view towards women and warfare, had him totally blind to the trap the young Queen was about to spring.

"Your Highness, planning this war is serious business, best left to experts and you do not need to worry yourself about such matters."

"I see," said the Queen through clenched teeth. "I suppose you mean experts such as my husband Ponnfarr?"

The Admiral grinned. "Yes, your Highness. Unfortunately your husband is a member of an off-world navy, so could not hold more than an advisory position on any war council."

"Prince Ponnfarr, my beloved husband," the Queen said sweetly, turning to him. "Your advice then on the Admiral's plans."

All eyes turned to Ponnfarr as he stood up. "You have fifty operational warships. With the battle plans and tactics the Admiral has put forward, you would have less than ten after the first attack, if you were lucky."

The Admiral started to speak, but the Queen cut across him.

"And have you reviewed my plans and tactics?" the Queen asked.

"Your plans are ambitious, but you have studied the tactics used by the Ick and it has a much greater chance of keeping your fleet intact," replied Ponnfarr.

"Good," continued the Queen. "As you have been released from service from the Fo'c'sle you are hereby appointed my first advisor and second in charge of the fleet, answering only to me. I am commander of the fleet and I will tell you all what the plans are. Any objection can be taken up with our royal champion, as is your right as Heeter nobles. Present your champions for trial by combat with mine, which would be my husband the Prince Ponnfarr. Does anyone wish to meet him in single combat, or is this silly matter closed?"The room remained silent as the officers quickly realised the queen had no intention of being a figurehead. With a final look around the room the Queen sat back down, indicating the meeting was over. After the last of the officers had left the Queen turned to Ponnfarr.

"Well?" she asked. "Pick fault in what I did. I'm sure this silly spoilt child got it all wrong."

"Your officers are not stupid. They will know you put forward the better plan. They will now follow your orders. They have no love for the Admiral, but he was their commander," Ponnfarr said honestly, secretly impressed by the plan she had put forward.

The Queen smiled, then innocently asked; "And you thought my plans were good?"

"When it comes to people's lives I won't lie for you. Your duty is to keep your men alive and win battles with as few casualties as possible. I said your plan was better as it was," Ponnfarr replied.

The Queen sat back hiding the smile on her face, the compliment and support from Ponnfarr pleasing her more than it should. For some reason she wanted his approval, and not just because he was a proven warrior. When he had called her a spoilt child it had struck a chord. Now she would make him see she was far more than that.

# CHAPTER 13

## Trading Lies.

### INTERSTELLAR NEWS CHANNEL 9.
### NEWS FLASH.

In business news it was today revealed that ninety-seven of the Inner Systems' top one hundred companies now fall under the Coffee Houses' conglomerate banner. Sixty per cent of the Federation are now employed by the Earth-based super-company with a further twenty per cent dependent on those companies The Federal Senate dismissed claims that the company had become too powerful, stating the difficult trading conditions during the war, and the collapse of fifteen of the old one hundred companies over the last few years distorted the list. A spokesman for the Federal Navy also praised the conglomerate, saying that without the unified trading power of the company the war effort would have been severely hampered.

Alienbutt sat in the pilot seat of the shuttle. He felt good to be space side again. Alongside him, the larger bulk of Stoney's ship matched his speed as they began to move out of the planet's orbit. Stoney had given him a list of contacts spanning over a dozen systems, many of them fellow traders who he trusted to help Alienbutt with information on systems further afield. They had decided the best course would be to jump between systems and gather information about any trouble in the systems he would need to cross.

He flicked a switch to open communication. "Stoney, all systems are good. I'm ready to go," Alienbutt said as he did a final visual check of the control panel.

"Don't forget to drop my name at your first couple of stops. It should get you better information," Stoney replied. "Good luck to you and I hope you make it home safe."

"Thanks, Stoney for all your help. Give my thanks again to the Princess and her parents," Alienbutt said as he saw Stoney's vessel stop and start to fall behind.

"And don't forget to be careful of Quint. He has the amulet that I brought through with me. It's one of his prized possessions so he won't give it up without a lot of persuasion. He is trouble but knows more about the Sharinta systems and beyond than anyone. You will need to get that information and the amulet from him. The amulet has to be the key to opening the portal for you to get home," Stoney finally said, just before Alienbutt hit the thrusters and shot forward. The ship headed into open space before disappearing in a flash as it jumped to light speed.

Alienbutt checked the flight data while absently sipping on a bottle of whiskey. Once happy he stood up and removed his butt plugs and placed them in a bowl of soapy water. Now would be a good time to give them a full service. While he waited for the plugs to soak, he pressed a couple of buttons on the replicator, and opening the hatch, lifted out the kebab that materialised. After all, he would need to test the butt plugs once they were cleaned. Sitting back down, he put his feet up onto the flight desk, farted out of his third arsehole and smiled as he began to eat. Finally he was heading home.

Alienbutt sat looking at the space station that was sitting in orbit above the planet. His first couple of stops had been uneventful, but here he was to meet with the trader called Quint, who Stoney had stressed was not entirely trustworthy. The space station was a large upturned cone with a large ring covered in solar panels attached by four struts to the point of the cone. Three large hangar bays were visible around the top of the station, but only two were lit up showing signs of occupancy. As he flew closer, his radio cracked to life.

"Unidentified craft, state your business and needs," a deep female voice demanded.

"This is Commander Alienbutt of the Ick Imperial Navy. I'm just passing through this sector and I am looking to do some trading for supplies with the trader known as Quint," Alienbutt responded, trying to sound official.

There was a pause before the woman responded. "There will be a security team awaiting your arrival in hangar two, and they will escort you to the offices of Quint. Follow the flight path that I am sending you now. Enjoy your visit."

Alienbutt shrugged and reached over to grab his boots from behind his seat where he had thrown them. The red boots were now looking very battered, and were missing more buckles than they had left. Looking around he saw an equally battered black kilt. Placing the boots on the empty co-pilot's chair he walked back and grabbed the kilt. In the weeks since he had left Stoney, he had taken to sitting around in the shuttle's cabin in just his pants and vest. Quickly he inserted his butt plugs and then put the kilt on. Returning to his chair he pulled on the boots. The ship's autopilot was following the course towards the space station. Finally he fastened his belt and placed his two handguns into the holsters. Fully dressed, he sat back down in the pilot's chair and took over control of the ship.

Crugack was the head of the station's small security force. His life was easy, as the station never usually had more than two or three trading vessels in at a time. His three-man team spent most of the time sitting around, but when Glarfel had picked up an unknown ship heading towards the station it caused a rush of activity in their office. Glarfel had been so excited that the ship was from an Imperial Navy but had managed to remain professional-sounding as she informed the ship of where to land. Crugack had been ordered to meet their visitor with a security detail. He would have a chance to show off his team to this obvious military officer, and maybe he would be the answer to their prayers. When he was younger he had dreamed of joining the military, but there was little call for soldiers unless he wanted to travel to the far systems and enlist in their endless wars, and that just sounded far too dangerous.

He stood in the hangar as the disappointingly small craft flew through the atmosphere shield and slowly moved to the bay indicated by the green flashing lights on the floor. Crugack inspected the craft. It had obvious weaponry attached, with a forward gun turret and what looked like some sort of torpedo tubes below. The ship hovered over the bay and landing gear unfurled as it touched down. Advancing with his three-man team, he was in position and waiting when the door to the craft opened and steps slid down. Puffing out his chest and pulling his shoulders back, he assumed his often practised military pose, throwing a quick look to his left and indicating with a nod of his head that the others should follow his lead. Their response was half-hearted and only achieved making them look slightly less slouched and crumpled. His was a race that had no history of military might and everything they knew of it had been learnt from visiting off world traders. Looking back to the ship he saw their visitor begin to walk down the steps and his chest deflated as he was unable to avoid the disappointed reaction to what he saw. As first impressions went, Alienbutt had just failed on all but one level. From the battered red boots, the strange strips of leather that made up his skirt, to the food-stained vest, he failed to impress. The belt with the two holstered handguns was the only thing that made this person look like he was a soldier. Finally getting past the strange outfit, Crugack took note of the metallic arm and the skeletal metal hand. Just maybe, he thought, this was a soldier. As the newcomer reached the bottom of the stairs, Crugack stepped forward and saluted.

"Welcome to Kalphella Station. Commander Alienbutt, is it?" Crugack said, wanting to ensure he was talking to the right person. He still did not want to think this strange large-arsed stranger could be a commander in an imperial navy.

Alienbutt grinned. "Nice to have a friendly welcome." He looked at the waiting security team. They were human-looking but had large barrel chests and long oval hairless heads. None of them carried a visible weapon but all wore a matching red uniform. "So are you the station security team that was to meet me?" he asked.

"I am Chief Crugack, head of the station security, and this is my team," Crugack said with a slight edge to his voice. Alienbutt looked past the chief at the rest of the team that were all looking at him, apart from the short one on the end, who seemed to have his eyes focused on the end of his nose.

"A very professional-looking squad you lead, Chief Crugack," Alienbutt lied smoothly, and saw the team straighten their stance, and the chief again puffed out his chest in pride.

"Thank you," replied Crugack with pride. "I informed the trader Quint of your imminent arrival. He says he is busy at the moment but you can wait to see him in his outer offices and he should be able to see you later today."

"Well if he is so busy, could you could just direct me to the market area? I will grab some fresh food. After being aboard ship with just replicator food I could do with a change and company. Maybe one of the other less busy traders would be open to doing business with the Ick Empire," Alienbutt said pleasantly, and saw a slight flicker in Crugack's eyes. He had guessed right that Quint was playing games and within minutes of him sitting down to eat would suddenly be free. "I was told to ask for Quint by the trader Stoney, but I'm sure one trader is as good as another." Alienbutt half-turned and pressed a button on his wrist-com. After a moment the doors to his ship began to close. Turning back he gave a smile and stood waiting.

"I'll take you up to the market myself. So, have you travelled far? We haven't heard of the Ick Empire before," Crugack asked, indicating they should walk, before turning to his squad. "Return to your duties. Glarfel would you inform Quint that our new arrival is heading for the market to get something to eat." Glarfel looked worried, but nodded her head. Being able to sense when things were not right was vital for a bounty hunter, and Alienbutt's senses began to wake up.

The market area was smaller than Alienbutt would have expected for a space station of its size, but was busy without being crowded. On the way up Crugack had spoken just about non-stop, asking questions that Alienbutt gave vague replies to. He had been shown to a food court area and had gone with the recommendation of a vender his host had suggested, so now sat at a table looking at the menu. Unable to read the menu he went with the tried and tested method of all strangers in strange lands; he looked at the pictures and searched for something that at least looked familiar. As a veteran of fast food outlets he knew full well that what would be put in front of him would look nothing like the fresh, crisp item in the picture. When his choice arrived, which in the picture vaguely resembled a burger, he said a silent prayer to Sung the One-eyed Lama that he wouldn't be poisoned. After the first bite he said a second prayer that he hoped he wasn't going to be poisoned. When Crugack's meal arrived, Alienbutt said his third prayer in as many minutes that he had not allowed Crugack to order for him. The security chief began to eat with relish a bowl of grey slime with what looked like lumps of fat floating in it.

Alienbutt noticed a change in the atmosphere of the room as voices became quieter. He looked up to see a new arrival in the food hall area. He was of a different species to the majority on the station who were from the planet below, Alienbutt presumed. He stood and looked around for a second and then his eyes found Alienbutt. Pushing his half-eaten burger into the middle of the table. Alienbutt watched him walk over. He was dressed in a dark green suit that matched his hair colour, while his skin was marble white. As he got closer Alienbutt noticed his intense bright red eyes and overlarge mouth that pulled back into a smile.

"Commander Alienbutt, I presume?" he said cheerfully, sitting down at the table. Alienbutt noticed Crugack stiffen slightly from the corner of his eye. "I apologise that I was busy when you arrived." Looking over to the waiter, he pointed to the table before returning his attention to Alienbutt. "I decided it was time for a little lunch, so thought I would introduce myself. I'm Quint, a humble trader, and I understand that you have a business proposal for me?"

"I need information and I was informed that you may be the most reliable source," Alienbutt said, sitting back in his chair.

"I have a large network of contacts, so I am well informed, If I do say so myself," Quint said, sitting forward and making a pyramid with his hands. "So what is the nature of this information?" Quint never removed his eyes from Alienbutt as the waiter came over and placed a bottle and two small cups on the table. "Would you care to join me for a drink while we talk?" he asked Alienbutt. "I would also invite our security chief to join us, but I'm sure we've kept him from pressing matters for far too long."

Crugack took the hint and quickly made his excuses. "Yes, I must get on, nice to have met you Commander." Alienbutt watched as he stood and almost bolted from the food court. Returning his attention to Quint, he saw he was still being studied.

"It seems the chief is a little in awe of you," Alienbutt observed.

"A very busy individual the chief is," Quint said, brushing away Alienbutt's statement as he poured a drink into each glass. "So, what information do you require? I'm sure we will be able to do business."

"My emperor is writing a book on religions of the universe, or some such thing. It's one of those things emperors do when they don't have a war to win. He wishes to be remembered after his passing, I suppose. He has heard of a strange cult that lives past the Sharinta systems and has dispatched me to gather information on them. What I need are star maps and information of any travel restriction that would be on my route." Alienbutt began, starting the story that he had worked out with Stoney and used with previous traders.

"You are on a fool's errand, Commander. No one visits that region of space and returns. That cult does not allow visitors," Quint said, taking a sip of his drink.

"Still, I am commanded to go there, and have travelled a great distance, too far to turn back now," Alienbutt said in mock sadness as he picked up the glass and took a sip. The drink was sickly sweet but left an after-burn to tell of its strength. "I cannot return home without my report and at the very least a couple of items of significance."

"If you enter that space you will not be returning home at all. They make sacrifices of any life-form that enters their space, and have been responsible for many raids along the borders of their space," Quint pressed. "If I give you the information, I am sending you to certain death."

Alienbutt picked up the bottle and poured two large measures and then downed his own. "If I go back without doing as commanded, I return to certain death. An emperor does not accept failure," he said sadly.

Quint refilled Alienbutt's drink. "I may be able to help you get around this little problem, but it will be expensive. Why don't we go back to my offices where we can talk in private?"

Alienbutt got unsteadily to his feet and looked around the room. He noticed that all the people who were native to the planet below sat with their heads down. All seemed nervous and tried their best not to be seen or see what was happening Only a couple of off-worlders were present and looked more like hired muscle than traders. Alienbutt had spent years as a taxi driver and then a bounty hunter and now his senses had not just woken up, they were screaming out that he was in trouble. He looked back at Quint and for a split second caught a look that confirmed that he was heading for trouble.

"If we are to talk business, then I need to return to my ship so I can pick up my trade goods. No point talking trade with nothing to show you," Alienbutt said, his head beginning to throb.

"There's no need for that. We can work out the details of our trade once you see what I have for you," Quint replied, giving an easy friendly smile.

"I'll be back in a few minutes, don't worry," Alienbutt said, and didn't wait for an answer. Alienbutt set off for the lift that would take him back to the hangar where his ship waited. He noticed the off-worlders begin to rise but then suddenly stop. Obviously Quint had ordered them to wait. As Alienbutt reached the lift, the doors slid open and he collided with the female security officer. With a snarl he pushed her back into the lift. "Get me to my ship or I'll kill you," Alienbutt hissed. The woman looked terrified, but nodded and pressed a button to close the door. Alienbutt was thankful that no one in the food hall would have been able to see into the lift, so wouldn't know of his hostage.

"What is going on and what the hell was in that drink?" Alienbutt said through clenched teeth, sweat pouring from his forehead.

"Quint has drugged you, it was the glass," Glarfel said in a terrified voice. "It's not our fault, him and his henchmen rule here. If we don't do as he says they will kill us and use their warships against the planet."

Alienbutt opened a small pouch on his belt and pulled out a small medi-syringe. Holding it to his neck, he pressed the button releasing the liquid into his bloodstream. "Let's hope Blackarachnia's hangover cure works on this drug too," he said to himself.

"If you were to lead us we would help you," Glarfel pleaded. "We don't know about how to fight, but you're a soldier; you could help us free ourselves."

Alienbutt began to feel better as the contents of the medi-syringe did its job. "Who are they and how many?" Alienbutt asked as the lift came to a stop.

"They are gun runners and smugglers, about thirty strong. They use our station here as their base because it's out of the way," Glarfel said quickly, hope lighting her face at the thought of possible help for her people.

As the doors opened and Alienbutt walked out into the hangar, he saw two of the off-worlders standing by his ship, using metal bars to try and open the door. Without thought Alienbutt pulled one of his handguns using his metallic arm and strode across the hangar towards them. He was halfway there before he was noticed. Dropping their tools, both scrambled to draw their own guns but neither made it as they joined their tools lying on the floor. Alienbutt looked down at his gun, he had used it without conscious thought. The targeting sensors on the wrist blinked an angry red. He looked back to the two dead off-worlders. Both had been shot through the head. Alienbutt shrugged and pressed the button on his wrist-com and the door to his ship opened. Without slowing he walked inside. Glarfel moved away from the lift nervously. She was shocked by the sudden casual violence that Alienbutt had just committed. Moments later Alienbutt reappeared carrying an assault rifle. He looked over to the only other ship in the hangar.

"Is that their ship?" he asked. Glarfel looked over and nodded. "Well if I was you I would duck," Alienbutt said and opened fire.

Explosions rocked the hangar as high explosive shells ripped through the unprotected ship. As the echoes died down and the space station's emergency systems began to spray foam onto the burning ship, Alienbutt turned to the security officer.

"I suggest you tell your people to make themselves scarce, as when I come out of my ship next I'm not stopping until Quint begs for his life. I can't stand people that put drugs in good alcohol." Alienbutt turned and walked to his ship, muttering, "Why can't I ever just go somewhere and be normal? Always the same, I end up been told I'm a saviour and then have to run around blowing things up. All I wanted was the star maps and Stoney's key so I can get home. I would have even traded fair for them."

Glarfel watched as Alienbutt disappeared onto his ship. When he was gone, she turned and ran.

# CHAPTER 14

## Fluffy Plots.

INTERSTELLAR NEWS CHANNEL 9.
NEWS FLASH.

A trade delegation today won a high court ruling for the easing of sanctions on space travel. The ruling will help ease shortages within the Inner Systems. The Federal Security council gave its backing to the delegation, saying the ruling will free up vital military units from ensuring the delivery of essential goods between planets. General Jee head of the Federation Navy and the Earth Defence Force stated that limited military escorts would be available where it did not interfere with operational security.

The ruling is seen by many to be a sign that the drawn out War of the Coffee Bean is coming to an end. With a decrease in terror attacks after a number of E.D.F. tactical strikes, and the Ick being unable to mount any new offensives, experts believe that a final push to end the war is not far off.

Geurick Tackful walked through the droid production facility. This was the main centre for the Federation's battle droids, a planet-wide factory producing a hundred thousand battle droids and over ten thousand robot fighter ships every twelve hours. It was a fully automated facility with less than a hundred people situated in the central control hub in case of any major problems that the maintenance driods could not fix. Now each of those support staff wore a little black box and all were under the control of Mr Fluffy. His new boss Mr Fluffy had not stopped at mind control on people; an entire new secret program had been added to the droids' database to be activated when Fluffy was ready to act. The Federation forces would find themselves surrounded by an army of mutinous droids right inside their own forces. Geurick was not happy at what he was seeing but he had little choice in his actions if he wanted to stay alive. On the bright side he had just successfully completed his latest mission and as a result soon the entire remaining Ick Fleet would no longer be a threat. Despite the fact that he now worked for Mr Fluffy, his main enemy was still the Ick, and he could in part justify his actions if he was working to bring them down.

Walking into the main control room, he saw the giant form of his new boss, the robotic battle suit of Mr Fluffy stood at over twelve feet in height and dwarfed everyone in the room.

"Was your mission a success, Tackful?" Mr Fluffy asked without turning to him.

"The data virus was uploaded into the relay system just like you ordered," replied Geurick, walking over to stand near to Mr Fluffy; but he was careful not to get close enough as to come within striking distance. Mr Fluffy was unpredictable and prone to lash out at the closest object.

"I have a final couple of tasks for you. After they are done I will be ready to act, and maybe give you your freedom back.

I will make you the greatest assassin the universe has ever known. You will have removed the Ick Navies and destroyed the heart of the Federation, leaving the path clear for the rise of a new order."

"You forget the Order of the Coffee Bean. They will still be a power even without the Federation," said Geurick. His loyalty to the secret order was far deeper rooted than he had thought. He took a step backward in case Fluffy reacted badly to his words. Fluffy turned slowly towards Geurick; instinctively the assassin's hand moved towards the pistol. This resulted in a loud purring noise coming from Mr Fluffy that Geurick had learnt was amusement. Suddenly Fluffy launched himself at Geurick. knocking him over. Before he had time to react, he was pinned to the floor and four razor-sharp claws were pressed to his throat.

"No one will be a threat to me anymore. I will stand alone as the only power in the universe. The days of Federations and Empires have passed; there will be only me and what I choose to allow."

Geurick lay very still, and waited for Mr Fluffy to spring to his feet again. There was a madness growing within his new boss, one that truly terrified the assassin.

"I have a package that you will deliver to the Federation Senate. I believe your order has a chapter house situated next to the Senate buildings where you can leave it for later collection," Mr Fluffy said as he got back to his feet. "And your secret order stopped being a threat weeks ago when our old friend Blackarachnia wiped out its ruling council. After his campaign of killing many of its operatives who ran the day to day business, he cut off its head. It is no longer in a position to function; it is leaderless and imploding as we speak. Its prophecy is all but destroyed, as is that of the Ick. They have not yet realised they have been replaced and no longer have a say in the future of the universe. There is now only me. I will say how the future is written." Mr Fluffy seemed to listen to something only he could hear and then screamed. "Alienbutt is gone! If the foolish oaf should somehow return it is too late, I will destroy him! He is no threat to anyone."

Geurick slowly climbed back to his feet, his shock at Mr Fluffy's outburst making him back off away from him. The news of the destruction of his order left him numb. He had allowed Blackarachnia to escape, and now the Order that had been the only family he knew had been destroyed.

"Very soon the two prophecies will be totally destroyed," Mr Fluffy continued in a calmer manner. "Already millions of my droids have been dispatched to the Federation fleet as they prepare for a new offensive against the Ick." Mr Fluffy turned and returned his attention to the giant screens showing different areas of the production facility as thousands of new droids were constantly being built.

"Your ship is being loaded with the crate. After you have delivered it, send a message to me and don't hang around on planet. You will not want to be late for the second part of your mission, and things may get a little heated around the Senate." Again Mr Fluffy began to purr, laughing at his own attempted joke, Geurick presumed. "After you make the delivery, you are to go kill whoever Wickede leaves in charge of the Ick while he flies off to his final battle. It will probably be his advisor Snoodgrass. Kill him and whoever is helping him keep the last of their people together."

Geurick nodded, eager to get out of the room. He was now sure Mr Fluffy was totally insane. He had studied his new employer whenever he was summoned for new orders, and he seemed to have two distinct personalities. The first was an amoral power-hungry control freak that thought the universe was just there for it to have something to stand on, while the second was an evil and twisted power-hungry control freak that wanted to destroy the universe because he could. As cats had become extinct shortly after humanity had first entered space, Geurick didn't realise the first personality of Mr Fluffy was quite normal for all cats, while the second would fit any cat in a bad mood.

Wickede sat reading the reports Snoodgrass had just brought him. All along the border of Ick space, the Federation had been quietly pulling their forces back. Snoodgrass's still extensive spy network had reported the same operation all along the front lines of Ashia Minor.

"Well, it looks like the Federation are wanting all their forces ready for a new offensive. Any clues yet on where?" Wickede asked, looking at his friend, who sat slumped in a chair opposite him.

"They are forming up well back from the front and my spies say that millions of new robotic units are being brought up, but no hint yet as to where they are going to strike."

Wickede shook his head. "Any hints from the book?" he asked, more in hope than anything else. Over the last few weeks, when all expected secrets to be revealed, the Book of Ick had gone silent, refusing to give any hints about what was to happen.

"Still nothing there, but Nifty is flying in, should be here in an hour or so. She's requested an immediate meeting, so I've ordered her to be escorted straight here and cleared your appointments for the rest of the day. From what I heard from Ramboe, she wasn't in the best of moods when she left his station, and a good few security officers needed medical attention."

Further conversation was cut short as the door opened and one of the monks of Ick came in, excited.

"We have found a passage in the Book!" Both Wickede and Snoodgrass sat up in their chairs and Wickede motioned the monk to continue. The Book of Ick was frustrating, as most of the time it was pure gibberish. Only at allotted times did a passage appear making sense, and then quite often it was cryptic.

"Brother Drick found this just now," he said excitedly. "After the blacke spider has caught its prey and cast the sun in their eye to smite all but the fist it starts the end. Thy enemy shall pull back and gather for a final time. A great battle will rage and many will be lost. As the battle rages all thy fate will be decided. A nexus will appear to force thy path, beware all is lost if your path is not true."

Snoodgrass stood up excited. "We know the Fist is Jee, so Blackarachnia must have gotten to the Orders high council. The Federation are withdrawing and preparing for a new offensive, a final battle." He looked over at Wickede, his face grim.

"Order all fleet to be ready to move within an hour's notice. For good or bad, it ends soon. There was a mention of Alienbutt. He was supposed to be here at the end and he's on his way," Wickede said grimly

Brother Drick looked troubled. "What does the last bit mean though, a nexus forces thy path? The book gives a direct warning, which is unheard of."

"Maybe it will reveal more? We must react to what it has told us. Let us know if you get anything else out of the book," Wickede said as he prepared to leave the room and take charge of the fleet. Brother Drick stood looking at the passage in the book. The last line worried him. It was a line that they had found a few times over the last couple of days, often unconnected to anything else. The book was sending a warning to them, but they didn't know what it was warning them about. Alienbutt was the nexus and his return would aid them; it didn't make sense even for the Book.

Hydroponic piloted the ship into a docking space on the Ick control station. All around them the Ick fleet looked a hive of activity.

"Something's got the Ick looking busy, Nifty. Do you think Wickede is getting some protection in after hearing what you did to Duke Ramboe's security force?"

"Very funny. It will be good to talk to civilised people again, you and those hunters are such Neanderthals." They had fallen into a tentative friendship over the last month based on small insults and Nifty complaining about Hydroponic's habit of smoking and leaving the toilet seat up.

"What's a Neanderthingy?" asked Hydroponic as he finished docking his ship and engaged the docking clamps. Nifty stood up and scowled down at him.

"How did Blackarachnia ever put up with you for so long?"

Hydroponic scratched at the stubble on his face, and without thinking reached and pulled a cigar out of his breast pocket. "Separate toilets and the fact we regularly got to blow things up and shoot people," he said with a shrug. "How did he put up with you?"

"You light that stinky thing and I'll shove it where the sun doesn't shine," Nifty warned him. Hydroponic returned the cigar to his pocket with a sigh.

The two disembarked and an Ick officer led them straight up to Wickede's office. Walking straight in Nifty took in the scene before her in an instant. Wickede lay on the floor holding his left arm, blood pumping through his fingers. Snoodgrass stood before him blocking a large figure in a long black cloak that held a small gun aimed at them. As they walked in the figure spun to face them bringing the gun to bear then stopped,

127

staggering back. His face was hidden beneath the hood of the coat. Hydroponic had his own pistol half drawn but Nifty spoke, stopping all movement in the room.

"What the bloody hell are you doing, you stupid fool?"

The figure's gun dropped from his hand, but still he didn't speak. All in the room remained still as Nifty walked forwards towards the would-be assassin.

"It's a good job the Book told me where to find you or where would we be?" She glanced over at Snoodgrass. "You'd better call for a medi team while I find out why my stupid bloody husband thought there was a need to shoot your Emperor." The figure slumped back and pulled back his hood, revealing his shocked face.

"You haven't been looking after yourself, and you're not eating enough. Look how skinny you're looking," Nifty continued scolding the bounty hunter. Finally she stood before him and stopped. "What's up, you not even got a hug for me? Typical, you bugger off gallivanting around without a word and just stand there like a naughty schoolboy when I finally catch up with you."

Blackarachnia seemed to finally focus on what was happening. "Nifty?" he managed to croak.

"It's me," she said, softly raising her hand to his face. "Now pull yourself together and explain to Wickede why you shot him. We will have a little talk about why you left me with that ape of a friend of yours later, and by talk, I mean you get to listen while I talk."

Blackarachnia looked over to Hydroponic and then nodded in response to Nifty's words, still in shock. "It was the voices, they told me Wickede killed Alienbutt."

Snoodgrass had helped Wickede to his feet, while the officer who had escorted them had gone to get a medi team. He looked up at Blackarachnia's words, and leaving Wickede to be led to a chair by Hydroponic, walked over to where Blackarachnia and Nifty stood.

"Please let me look at your eyes, Blackarachnia," he said, pulling out a small device from his belt and gently moving Nifty so he stood in front of the bounty hunter. He held it up to his eyes and pressed a button, switching on a green light.

"We need to get you to the medi bay too. Someone tried mind control on you at some point. It failed but left a link to your subconscious for them to send you instructions. You've been getting subliminal messages trying to urge you to do things. I had this little device made after the assassination attempt on Commander Kali, as I thought it would come in useful."

"Mr Fluffy," Nifty stated. "It has to have happened when you were in stasis."

Turning back to Wickede, Snoodgrass smiled. "Looks like you can't have him arrested for shooting you. We'll get you both sorted, then we need a full command meeting."

Geurick Tackful landed his ship in the deserted hanger bay. This was the main chapter house for his Order, and the lack of activity was worrying. As he walked down a ramp a couple of novices ran over to greet him.

"What is happening?" he asked when they reached him. "Where is everyone?"

"The Order is on full alert, sir, everyone is out in the field. The Grand Master asks if you would see him in his quarters. We didn't know if you had survived until you contacted us to say you would be arriving," said one of the novices. He was wearing a dark grey uniform rather than the black of those fully trained. To leave only partly trained assassins to protect the main chapter house of their Order showed that things had indeed gone wrong.

"Very well. There is a crate in my ship's hold. Have it transferred to my quarters." With that he walked off to meet with the Grand Master.

As Geurick marched through the silent chapter house, he was shocked by the fact that almost no staff remained, only a handful of novices and domestic robots. Quickly he reached the Grand Master's office and knocked; after a moment he was bid to enter. The Grand Master had once been a powerful man but age had robbed him of the necessary skills to work in the field. He now sat behind his desk looking even older than Geurick remembered.

"Geurick, we didn't know what had happened to you, just that you had been given a contract by a member of the high council. I am glad you're still alive," said the Grand Master in greeting, a look of relief on his face. The man had been close to a father figure to the students he had spent the last fifteen years training since becoming leader of the Order.

"Grand Master, what has happened? I've heard rumours, but I've been out of touch with all while on my hunt."

The Grand Master indicated a chair for Geurick to sit.

"The High Council are all dead, as are many of our senior agents. Only Jee is still alive, and he has ordered all operatives into the field to act as protection for him and to hunt for Blackarachnia. He will be pleased that you can join the hunt."

Geurick sagged in the chair. Mr Fluffy had told the truth about the High Council. The Grand Master continued. "The Order is all but crippled. We must finish the war, so to that end Jee is massing the entire Federation Navy to strike in the next month. He has been bolstered by new robotic forces and is ready to strike. The prophecy is making no sense; it speaks of the nexus and the destruction of the Ick, but also of a great disaster. We are working blind and fighting for our lives. It has

given us nothing of use since warning of the Heeter uprising."
The Grand Master paused, the strain of events evident on his
face. "Your return gives me hope that we will survive. Will
you be leaving to join up with your brothers? I know it would
lift their hearts too to stand with the best of our order in the
coming days."

Geurick was tempted to stand and fall with the last of his
people but he shook his head. "I have a last task to complete
before I can join up them, I only stopped by here as I need
some equipment from my quarters."

"Then I have delayed you long enough, Geurick. You are
the finest of our chapter and I hope you live long enough to
replace me when our Order rises again to rule the universe."

Geurick nodded and stood up. "Thank you Grand Master,
your words mean a great deal." He paused for a second ready
to give warning but felt an itching inside his brain, building as
quickly as the thought had come to him. Turning quickly he
left. He would finish Mr Fluffy's orders and then spend the
rest of his life hunting down Blackarachnia and everyone the
bounty hunter had ever met, and that included Mr Fluffy.

# CHAPTER 15

## The Battle for Kalphella Station.

### INTERSTELLAR NEWS CHANNEL 9.
### NEWS FLASH.

Rumours circulating of a build-up of Federal forces have been dismissed as false and just normal operational rotation. A spokesman from the Federal Navy said that a number of fleets that have been reported to be moving up to the front lines are being repositioned to avoid detection from Ick spies. The prolonged stand-off between the two forces has led to more muted calls for peace talks but during discussions in the Senate such ideas were dismissed while skirmishes continued.

In other news the family of Trescoplaphones at the centre of a bidding war after the collapse of the Loc Ness Olde Scotland theme park have been sold to the J.O. School Dinners for Olde Britannia plc. Despite objections from environmentalists the big beasties are heading for the dinner table.

As the rumbling of the explosions finished Quint had ordered all his off-worlders to him. Now over thirty had gathered in the food hall of the market, all armed and ready. Quint had underestimated the stranger Alienbutt. The fact that he had been able to not only walk, but work out what was happening with the amount of the drug he had spiked the drink with should not have been possible. Somehow he had made it back to his ship and killed two of his men, before seriously damaging one of his trading ships. Then, just to make a bad day worse, the main lighting had failed. That had sparked a mass panic amongst the locals who had run for the relative safety of their quarters on the lower levels, removing his civilian shield. The emergency lighting had quickly kicked in giving a dull red light just bright enough to see. Quint looked around at his band of men. Each one was handpicked for their ruthlessness and violent tendencies. Picking out his number two he beckoned him over.

"Tarnic, pick ten men and take the steps up to the hangar. Wait for my signal then you go in all guns," Quint ordered.

"The stairs? But there's about four thousand between here and the hangar," Tarnic complained. Without warning Quint backhanded him across the face, making him stagger back.

"I'm not interested in how many steps there are. I just want you up there and don't damage his ship, I want the weaponry off of it," Quint shouted in fury at being questioned. Tarnic quickly backed off to gather up the men to take the stairs. Quint's attention then fell upon Crugack, who stood cowering off to one side.

"You had better have some good news for me, Crugack," he warned.

"He is still in the hangar but the explosions have knocked all the security cameras offline. We're still working to reboot them," Crugack said nervously, looking to the floor.

"Tell me, why do I keep you around?" Quint asked calmly, recovering his temper. Crugack didn't answer, unsure of what to say. "No I don't know either." With that Quint pulled out his gun and shot the security chief in the head. He walked over to the body and looked down at the dead Crugack. "Belorid, give it ten minutes then take five men up the lift," he ordered, never taking his eyes from the man he had just murdered.

Glarfel had reached the security room just in time to see the events in the food hall. She looked in horror at the monitor. Alienbutt had scared her with his act of sudden violence but this was worse. She had dreamed of being free of the oppression of Quint and his thugs but now they had a chance, the violence was too real. She reached for the microphone and quickly opened a channel to Alienbutt's ship.

"Commander Alienbutt, are you there?" She got no response. "Alienbutt please, they just murdered Crugack." Again she got silence and slumped down into the chair, tears running down her face.

"I'm sorry, he didn't deserve that," Alienbutt's voice came over the radio.

"There's a group of them coming up the stairwell to you. What should I do?" she asked, wiping the tears from her eyes.

"Do you have an oxygen mask?" Alienbutt asked.

"Yes, we have small respirator tanks in case of emergency, why?" Glarfel asked in confusion. She'd expected to be asked about having weapons.

"Get the tank and lock your door. If you can seal off the air supply to the rest of your people, they'll thank you for it," Alienbutt said, then she heard a pinging sound. "Got to go, my kebabs are ready. Just stay in your security office."

Alienbutt pulled out the kebabs and poured a large measure

of chilli sauce over them. For some reason replicator kebabs were not spicy enough. Putting a small bag over his shoulder, he slung the rifle over his other arm and grabbed the kebab and a fresh whiskey bottle. Alternating between eating the kebab and taking drinks from the whiskey bottle, he left the ship and headed across the hanger to the lift doors. By the time he reached them the kebab was gone, as was half the whiskey bottle. Unslinging the bag he opened it and pulled out a small metal sphere. Twisting it in both hands, it split into two. He placed one half on each of the lift doors then pulled a cord from one and carefully connected it to the other. Picking up the bag he then walked over towards the stairway door. Reaching the door Alienbutt drank the last of the whiskey and stood looking around for somewhere to put the empty bottle. After a moment he smiled to himself and placed it over his arsehole number two. A small leak later the bottle had a green tinge inside. He quickly put the lid back on. Carefully he opened the door and listened; from down the stairwell he heard the sound of movement. Bending down he placed the bottle on the floor and rolled it towards the top step and unslung the rifle from his back. The bottle rolled off the top step and started to noisily bounce down the steps. The sound of movement stopped. The stairwell was circular with the stairs going around the outer walls, the bottle bounced down and then Alienbutt heard the sound of it breaking. After a moment he heard sound again from the people coming up the stairs as they cursed and began to throw up. Alienbutt smiled at the attackers' discomfort, then noticed his robotic arm begin to move. He watched confused as it reached into his bag and pulled a small thermal grenade out. Pressing a button on the top of the grenade the metallic hand set the timer then using the same method it rolled the grenade down the stairs. Alienbutt jumped up and moved back into the hangar, closing the door. He looked down at his arm, looking to see what it would do next. He set off back towards his ship, his robotic arm held out in front of him, carefully watching for any more movement, but it acted normally, giving the impression that it had not done anything. He was halfway back to his ship when the grenade exploded. As the echoes died of that explosion he heard the ping of the lift arriving. Alienbutt turned and saw the doors begin to open, the lift full of people. The cord connecting the two halves of the sphere snapped. Alienbutt dived for cover, expecting an explosion. After a moment he lifted his head to see the five off-worlders run out of the lift and begin to fire their guns at him. Caught in the open, Alienbutt's metallic arm, still holding the assault rifle, reacted and returned fire, causing his attackers to dive for the floor as the high velocity rounds ripped into the wall and lift doors. One hit the intended booby trap and a giant fireball ripped across the hangar. Again the station's safety system sprang to life, spraying foam down to smother the flames.

Alienbutt sat up. He was covered in foam, his hair and clothing singed by the fireball. Looking over towards the lift he picked out the bodies of the assailants lying on the floor, smoke rising from their foam-covered bodies. The lift doors were ripped apart, the mangled edges still glowing red and pinging as they cooled. Only the distance and fact that he had been lying down had prevented him from being caught up in the inferno of the booby trap's blast.

"Damn, next time I'll read the instructions, not just look at the pictures," Alienbutt said to himself. Getting back to his feet he reached into his bag and pulled out a fresh bottle of whiskey. Opening the lid, he took a drink. After half draining the bottle he looked down at his metallic hand.

"When this is over, me and you are having a talk." The hand gave him a thumbs-up. "Oh Sung, please let this be a bad trip from Quint's drugs," Alienbutt said, before pressing a button on his wrist-com as he lifted his arm to speak. "Glarfel, are you there?"

"Commander Alienbutt, what's going on? There's explosion and fire alarms going off all over around the hangar."

"Just introducing myself to Quint's men. You need to patch me through to wherever Quint is; I think I should talk to him," Alienbutt asked. After a moment Glarfel said she was ready.

Quint stood waiting with the remaining members of his men. The sound of an explosion had rocked the stairwell, while the lift had reached the hangar and then gone out of service. With no response from any of his men, those remaining had started to quietly murmur amongst themselves and he knew they were nervous. Suddenly Crugack's radio crackled to life. Bending down he picked it up.

"Who is this?" he asked angrily.

"I'm the person who is going to destroy this little operation you have running here, because you murdered the Kalphella Station's security chief and also because you tried to drug me," the voice said.

"Alienbutt, what madness is this? Where are my men?" Quint hissed, turning away from his men who were still in the food hall.

"Well, the ones you sent up in the lift are toast while the ones in the stairwell are just as dead, but more shredded and then toasted. Now I'm coming to get you," Alienbutt answered. "I came here to trade, but you started a fight."

"You can't possibly think you can beat us all, Alienbutt." Quint heard a disturbance behind him and lowered the radio. "Stop that noise and get yourself ready, I want this creep dead," Quint shouted without turning. "And what the hell is that smell?" Finally he turned around to see his remaining men all lying on the floor, unconscious.

"Sorry that's me, I farted," Alienbutt said from the stairwell door, his assault rifle pointed at Quint. "Now we are going to discuss getting the star maps and also the amulet that you obtained from the trader Stoney."

"They're in my office," Quint said, coughing and falling to his knees at the effects of Alienbutt's fart. "We can make a deal," he pleaded.

"The punishment for killing a Kalphella security officer under the treaty of the Ungarian alliance is death," Alienbutt said without emotion. "I looked it up."

"But the Ungarian alliance hasn't existed for five hundred years," Quint said, panicking.

"Don't know about that. The law, though, was never repealed." Alienbutt walked over to stand above Quint and suddenly smashed him in the face with the butt of the rifle. "It's your lucky day though, I don't kill unarmed people."

Alienbutt sat in Quint's office, looking at the star maps on the computer screen. On the table beside him was a strange golden amulet. The information on this strange cult that controlled the part of space where the gateway was located was scarce, as very few people had ever gotten out of there alive to say what was there. Over hundreds of years the civilisations that survived had tried on a few occasions to put an end to the cult, but all attempts had failed and the large navies that had sailed off to wage war had never returned. Then again, Alienbutt knew that he could take over the entire universe here with half a dozen Ick dreadnoughts. The majority of the locals seemed much too smart to bother with war, and those that did seem to enjoy a fight were more gifted amateurs than professional soldiers.

Glarfel walked into the office and stood nervously until

Alienbutt looked up and gave a half smile.

"Do you have them locked up?" Alienbutt asked, sitting back in the chair.

"Well erm," she began. "We don't actually have any cells, so Corporal Covans suggested putting them in one of the airlocks as you can't open them from the inside and we never use them anymore."

"Very inventive solution, good on the Corporal for his great idea," Alienbutt said, knowing these people were out of their depth with what had occurred and would struggle to contain the threat Quint and his off-worlders still posed.

"There was a slight problem," Glarfel said quietly, looking at the floor. "There was some sort of malfunction and the space side door to the airlock opened. There was nothing we could do to save them."

Alienbutt looked at the computer screen. Minimizing the star charts, he closed a second window headed 'Kalphella safety overrides' and deleted the computer browsing history. "Well, accidents sometimes happen Glarfel, most likely a glitch due to the explosions and stuff that went on," Alienbutt said innocently.

"Did you get what you needed from Quint's computer to help you get home?" Glarfel asked. Alienbutt had explained the reason for his arrival after the fight.

"Yes, thank you, although information on the cult is sketchy at best." Alienbutt said, standing up and picking up the amulet.

"And with the terrible accident that befell Quint, there's no legal reason to impound Quint's possessions until a trial so you may as well take the amulet if it helps you," Glarfel said with a knowing smile.

"That's good, time really is against me," Alienbutt said, returning the smile. "And Quint and his men are no longer a threat to your people. Seems we both win."

"When you leave, plot a course for the library at Watakusha Prime, it's a little out of your way but it holds over three thousand years of knowledge. If anyone knows about what you will face they will," Glarfel said, and Alienbutt realised he was been asked politely to leave.

"Thank you, I'll head out there," he said, walking around the desk. Glarfel continued to look at the floor, unable to meet his eyes as he left.

Alienbutt waited until he was into deep space before he brought his ship to a stop and looked down at his arm.

"OK you, I want an explanation. What the hell was going on back there with that grenade and all that?" The arm showed no sign of responding and after a minute Alienbutt began to feel foolish. "Well, that's better, last thing I need is an arm that does its own thing." Alienbutt looked away from the arm then looked back out of the corner of his eye to see if it moved. Despite it not doing anything, Alienbutt wasn't convinced. His arm was not right and he didn't trust it.

# CHAPTER 16

## Sympathy for the....

### INTERSTELLAR NEWS CHANNEL 9.
### NEWS FLASH.

The Federal Security Council today confirmed that the Senate elections will not go ahead during this time of trouble within the Federation. The nine-yearly general elections have taken place without fail since the creation of the Federation of planets a thousand years ago. In a short statement to the Senate the Security Council spokesperson stated that the safety of the voters could not be guaranteed at this time and stability was essential at this critical time in the Federation history. An election would cause too much disruption to the vital task the Senate has in running the Inner Systems Federation. The news has sparked some protests with radical political groups claiming that this is the first move to end democracy. Security forces have moved quickly to disperse gatherings and on a few planets martial law has been declared.

Frank walked down the corridor. This wasn't the corridor to his laboratory, although it was much like it. He stopped to consider what was different. It looked identical, even down to the smoke damage from the fire he had started last week when one of his experiments had not worked quite right. On the bright side he had invented a liquid that once burning could not be put out until it was consumed. He had sent his findings to the weapons department, as the litre of fluid had burnt for three days and made a hole clear through the steel floor and into the bedrock beneath it that was almost thirty feet deep. The fumes released had also made working without a hostile environment suit impossible, but it was another failure, as he searched to reproduce Alienbutt essence. Brussels sprout chilli fed to a Kweglarian Swamp beast (the closest known digestive system to the Alienbutt's) had been removed from the list of possible replacements. The gas produced was bad, but of no use as a fuel additive; but extracting the beast's urine could provide the basis for a great new warhead for Ick missiles.

Frank walked up to the doors to his laboratory and they slid open. As he walked in, the alarms went off. Frank cursed at the noise made by the Ick alarm, a kind of whoo whoo noise that he found grating. As he started to walk over to the main control panel to switch them off, he noticed that this certainly wasn't his laboratory. All the experiments were the same, but it was far too ordered, and he had never used tablecloths and scatter cushions. He noticed Kirk over to one side, standing with a feather duster, looking puzzled at what to do with it. He was about to go over and ask him about the sudden soft furnishings, when he saw a second figure. As the wail of the alarm continued, the slight figure in strange clothing grinned and then struck a strange pose that involved thrusting out his hips and then swinging one leg up to rest on a table. The figure then blew a kiss in Frank's direction and did a strange wiggle with his shoulders. Frank turned to see if anyone was stood behind him but with dismay he realised, apart from Kirk, he was alone. The very odd stranger then waited until he had Frank's full attention again and then he began to speak.

"Please allow me to introduce myself, I'm a man of wealth and taste."

Frank struggled to listen to the effeminate voice as it was drowned out by the wailing alarm, but the stranger kept talking. "I've been around for a long long time." Frank reached over and turned the alarms off. "So many men have seen my face." The figure paused as the alarm stopped. "Bugger, do you realise how long I've been setting up this entrance? And you've ruined it," he moaned, putting his hands on his hips and pouting. Frank looked around confused, as he was totally out of his depth of social interaction. From a few episodes of one of Kirk's space series that he insisted on showing to Frank he realised that when a female tried to catch the hero's eye they sometimes acted like this.

"Erm, sorry, but I couldn't hear you properly for the alarm."

"Do you realise how much trouble I had getting hold of this vintage Prada outfit and ensuring that the right alarms were fitted to your laboratory?" The figure stood tapping one foot doing his best to look annoyed. Frank looked at his feet, more to avoid laughing at the figure and his ridiculous pose than feeling regret for turning off the alarms.

"Sorry, I can turn the alarm back on if it helps, and what's Prada?"

The figure strutted forward towards Frank shaking his head and waving one hand in a dismissive manner. "It's too late now, you just ruined the moment." He stood before Frank and looked him up and down. "You really need to work on your image. Just because you're a scientist you don't have to look so..." He trailed off and stood lost for words for a moment and he inspected Frank. Finally he came to a decision. "You need a makeover boyfriend, and seriously, you never heard of Prada?" He stood as if hearing someone speak. "OK, I'm not getting distracted, he's just being difficult and not following my script." He paused. "I so gave you a script for this so my entrance would leave an impression." Frank followed where the stranger was looking and realised he was holding a conversation with the air about six feet above his head.

"Sorry to interrupt but I've not seen any script," Frank said quietly. The stranger stopped talking and crossed his arms in disgust.

"Right, Frank, you're dreaming, we are all dreaming this dream and I'm here to tell you how to get Alienbutt back."

Frank rubbed his chin as he considered this. As strange as it all seemed, he found himself accepting what was happening, but as a scientist he had to ask questions.

"Right, but if this is a dream is Kirk here too or just part of my dream? It's just that robots don't dream and I never had a robot in my dreams before, well apart from one time when..."

"No! Don't go there!" cut in the stranger desperately. "I can feel an emotional scar on a collision course if you continue with that train of thought."

"There was this pleasure droi..." Frank trailed off to silence, so the stranger continued, choosing to ignore thoughts of Frank's robotic dream.

"When my brother's involved, everything dreams, and dreams can become real. So Kirk is here to tell you what happened when you wake up so you know it's all true. Clever trick that, isn't it?"

Frank thought about this for a moment and quickly he worked out a mathematical calculation that would support the stranger's words about Kirk being able to dream. He then shrugged and accepted it.

"So you know how to get Alienbutt back? And you're just going to tell me?" Frank looked around as something caught his eye. "You put oriental screens into my laboratory? And white scatter rugs?" Frank looked around further at the strange additions.

"Have you noticed the diamanté lampshades? I carried the theme through to the new chandeliers too," put in the stranger with pride, as Frank continued to look around. The strange man stood jumping up and down, clapping his hands excitedly as Frank noticed each new feature.

"And did you just turn my lab coat pink and put lace frills on the cuffs too?" asked Frank.

The stranger smiled, still jumping up and down. "Look at your shoes, look at your shoes," he begged.

Frank looked down to see bright red glittery pointed shoes where his worn brown loafers should be. "Alienbutt told me about you. You're Fashion, aren't you?"

The stranger grinned even wider. "I just knew you would love them. I saw you and thought, now this is a man that knows style. Look, my brother is giving me grief about telling you the plan, so let me get that out of the way and then we can talk shop."

Quickly Frank was told what he would need to do and where he would need to go.

"Now we got the dull stuff out of the way I really need to sort out your look and that bushy beard is so not working, hello, caveman chic is old."

"You touch my beard and I'll burn the scatter cushions," Frank warned. Fashion staggered back as if he had been slapped, his arm rising in an overdramatic way to fend off an invisible blow.

"You are so mean," He gasped, tears in his eyes.

Kirk walked forward and stood looking at the two. He knew he had advanced far beyond what he should be; he could think for himself, for a start. Not the usual robot reactions of responding to programmed variables, but actual thoughts, and he could learn new things. Since appearing in this dream he had been trying to work out what it was. Failing, he now decided that he had to warn Frank about the stranger. He looked at Frank and saw a scruffy human who while strange, was still human. But the other being was not human, although it tried to appear that way. Kirk looked at the figure that to his single robot eye looked human, but with the entire mass of a black hole held within its form trying to burst out.

"I'm sorry to interrupt," he started, and both turned and looked down at him, so he continued. "I can order the things needed for this plan. I feel it's got a good chance of working, based on the evidence that it comes from beings from outside our time and dimension, but that said, this is the being that did a makeover on Alienbutt, so I wouldn't trust him on fashion tips. You should not trust this being with anything beyond the important science things."

The figure's mouth dropped open, a look of outrage on his face. After half a dozen attempts, he finally spoke.

"How rude is your robot? You are both so hurtful. Alienbutt is a style icon to millions all over the universe. The style he sets will echo down the centuries." He put his hands onto his hips and looked away in disgust.

Frank looked from Kirk to the stranger before speaking. "Alienbutt is a style icon? Is there two of him? The one I know wears girl's boots and a skirt and looks a right fart. If he ever sobers up and realises what he looks like, he'll die of shame."

The stranger's hand snaked out and slapped Frank across the face. "You're so mean. Why I bother I don't know. I'm not staying here any longer."

With that he disappeared. Frank looked down at Kirk.

"If this is real then I'm giving up on science, as his way of getting Alienbutt back is the stupidest thing I've ever heard."

Kirk tried to shrug his shoulders. It was impossible for him to do so; he ended up doing a little hop.

"We are talking about Alienbutt here, so you may need to see a careers advisor in the morning." Kirk looked at Frank. "And don't wear that pink coat you've got on. It may badly influence the jobs you're offered."

Frank looked around the lab and saw a large couch in one corner. "Well that couch could be a good idea. It looks real comfortable. What do you think, Kirk?"

Kirk cocked his head to one side. "Did you keep any pictures of that pleasure droid?" Frank looked down at Kirk and blushed, realising suddenly how wrong that dream had been. Quickly he changed the subject.

"We need to get hold of a science ship and crew." He picked up a fluffy scatter cushion. "Have these ever been of any practical use?"

# CHAPTER 17

## Cybercore's Smartchip.

INTERSTELLAR NEWS CHANNEL 9.
NEWS FLASH.

The planetary university of Rocthorpe reopened today as a military training academy. The Federation's brightest students will now receive state of the art teaching in the new look higher education facility that will split their education between military training and chosen scientific modules.

The university was closed down after it was discovered that many of the professors were using their position to recruit students into an anti-federation terror squad. Their leader Squegal Quinch was found guilty of high treason and the university was closed during violent riots.

The new head of the university General Tratum Hockstum, a professor of military tactics, has spoken of his hope of a new generation of elite personnel committed to defending the ideals of the Federation in the post war universe. General Hockstum returns to public life after being cleared of any involvement in the Cybercore project T mind control scandal.

The library at Watakusha Prime was the largest collection of information known in any universe. Everything from two thousand year old shopping lists for groceries to a formula to guarantee divine intervention could be found there. If it had been written down and somehow survived, then it was in the library. Over five million librarians lived within the library that covered an entire continent of the planet. The rules of the library were simple; if you wanted information you had to give information back, and a printed copy of the book of Ick had gotten Alienbutt a meeting with the head of religious writings.

The librarian had flicked through the book and smiled before laying it down on the table between them. "I am informed you seek information on the Wantooaninyougo Temple," he said, smiling.

"I've been informed there is a gateway there. I can use it to get home," Alienbutt said. "Everything I have heard so far about it makes me think they don't like visitors, so any information that will help me reach the gateway would help."

"The gateway and temple have been there for as long as our records go back; it is the most ancient site known to us. We believe it is the last remaining site of a once great empire that travelled between universes and planes of reality using that gateway. Fortunately the present priests of Wantooaninyougo have no idea how to use the portal. They are, we believe, the direct descendants of that once great empire, and it is thought those high up in the priesthood have discovered the secret of immortality." The librarian stood up and walked over to a wall full of books and picked one out. "Much of what we have learnt cannot be verified, as very few people ever escape the temple, unless you count having your heart cut out and then your body being thrown into the void of the gateway, as escape."

"I would sooner keep my heart where it is when I pass

through the gateway. I'm going to need it on the other side," Alienbutt replied as the librarian put the slim book on the table.

"This is the account of all those we know of who have escaped the Wantooaninyougo temple. The accounts go back almost two thousand years," he said with pride. As he opened the book, Alienbutt saw that it was actually a case. Inside was a small silver disk that the librarian placed into a slot on the table. A holo-screen appeared above the table.

"Only a handful of people have ever escaped and they paint a picture of an evil place. Many have tried to destroy the priesthood but all have failed, so when the priests go hunting for sacrifices everyone hides."

"So the surrounding systems are not devout to their beliefs. That will help me get through to the right place without interference or reinforcements turning up. How often do the priests go out raiding?" Alienbutt asked.

"You cannot be planning to do battle! The priests cannot be defeated by force of arms. They have destroyed entire navies," the librarian said in shock.

"No offence, but I've seen the warships here and I could destroy entire navies on my own. According to your book here the last fleet to try was over five hundred years ago. What did they set off in, wind up ships?" Alienbutt asked, smiling.

"So you have a plan to defeat the priests of Wantooaninyougo?" the librarian asked.

"A very good plan, based on an ancient general of the Olde highlanders of Hardstool called William Wallys, or something like that. I'm going to drink a load of whiskey, eat lots of kebabs and go pick a fight."

"You plan to take on the most evil and powerful force known in our universe single-handed?" the librarian said aghast, still not believing what he was hearing.

Alienbutt looked down at his metallic arm. "It's not considered polite to point out the synthetic arm."

Alienbutt sat in the pilot's chair with his feet resting on the control desk as he absently sipped on a bottle of whiskey. He was sitting on what was considered the border of Wantooaninyougo space, the wrong side of safe flying, but not quite into aggressive suicide flying. He had chosen his position carefully, as this seemed to be the main route in and out of Wantooaninyougo space for their raiding fleets. He had been sitting waiting for about an hour before he was finally hailed. Leaning over his flipped the communication switch.

"Unknown craft, this is the Farlian early warning base. You are about to enter dangerous space. Please be advised that you should turn around and leave," a voice said nervously.

"Good, I'm in the right place then. So do you have any idea when those mad priests are doing their next collection run?" Alienbutt asked holding up the whiskey bottle to inspect it. After a moment of swirling the contents around he took another drink.

"You want to meet the Wantooaninyougo priests?" the voice asked, sounding shocked. "Are you mad? Do you know what they do to people?" it added after a pause.

"Do you know what they do? And it's not what they do that's important," Alienbutt said, reaching over to a half-eaten kebab and picking out a piece of meat. Alienbutt's long range sensors picked up two ships on an intercept course heading out of Wantooaninyougo space. "Now if you don't mind, I need to concentrate on getting their attention," Alienbutt said as he swung his legs down and prepared himself. As the ship got closer Alienbutt began to hail them but his attempts were ignored. As the ships came within visual range Alienbutt's metallic arm decided to wake up, and pressed the button to fire one of his torpedoes. It streaked forward and hit the ship on the left. The ship disappeared in a string of explosions as the second ship veered away.

"What in Sung's name are you doing?" Alienbutt shouted, screaming at his hand in shock.

The priest's ship swung around and came to a stop, holding position off to Alienbutt's left. After a moment they opened communication.

"You have attacked the envoys of the exalted Grandmaster Lucifus, anointed leader of the Wantooaninyougo."

"Erm, sorry about that, had a little hardware malfunction," Alienbutt replied, then watched in horror as his metallic hand fired off a second torpedo. Alienbutt jumped up and grabbed the first aid box with his real hand. Flipping open the lid he pulled out a laser scalpel.

"Right then, you..." He stopped dead as he felt the end of his pistol barrel touch his chin. Keeping very still he moved just his eyes to look down to see the robotic arm holding the pistol. Alienbutt dropped the laser scalpel and after a moment the pistol was removed. "You had better start telling me what is going on, arm, or I swear to Sung I will..." Alienbutt stopped, as he had no idea what he could do. The arm was a part of him. "Well I'll think of something."

A small screen popped up on his metallic forearm.

```
THEY WERE ENEMIES, ENEMIES MUST BE
             DESTROYED.
```

Alienbutt read the message with disbelief. "Who and what the hell are you?" he asked.

```
         CYBERCORE SMARTCHIP MRK8
    PROTOTYPE. TOTAL ANNIHILATION MODE
    ACTIVATED. AUTOMATIC HOST OVERRIDE
    ENABLED. DEADLY FORCE AUTHORISED.
```

Alienbutt shook his head. "You can't keep killing people like this. I'm not a murderer. What you are doing is wrong." The screen went blank for a while as lights flashed within the metallic casing of the arm.

TOTAL ANNIHILATION MODE ACTIVATED.
SYSTEMS OPERATING WITHIN PROGRAM
PARAMETERS.

"I don't want total annihilation mode. You are killing everyone, and don't think I'm going to forget about you putting a gun to my head either," Alienbutt insisted. "Replacement arms aren't supposed to do that. You do what I want when I say."

YOU HAD BECOME IRRATIONAL.

"You had just blown up two ships!" Alienbutt said in disbelief.

I WAS TRYING TO HELP.

"Well, don't. In future when it comes to combat you do nothing until I say, is that clear?" Alienbutt ordered, raising his voice.

UNDERSTOOD.

The screen again went blank and lights again began to flash. After a moment the lights went out.

CYBERCORE SMARTCHIP MRK8
PROTOTYPE. PLEASE CHOOSE ACTIVITY
MODE. FOR ASSASSINATION SAY 1, FOR
SHOCK TROOPER SAY 2, FOR GENERAL
USE SAY 3. FOR TOTAL ANNIHILATION
MODE SAY 4.

Alienbutt looked at the screen as he sat back down into the pilot's chair. After a moment's consideration he answered.

"Three."

AUTOMATIC HOST OVERRIDE ON OR OFF?

"Definitely on," Alienbutt answered.

DEADLY FORCE AUTHORISATION ON OR
                        OFF.

"Best keep that on, I suppose," Alienbutt said after a moment's consideration.

THANK YOU FOR CHOOSING CYBERCORE.
PLEASE ENJOY YOUR NEW ARM.

With that the screen disappeared back into the arm. Alienbutt moved his robotic arm experimentally and wiggled his fingers. Checking the scanners and sensors Alienbutt prepared to head forward into Wantooaninyougo space.

"Can I ask you something, arm?" Alienbutt asked, but the screen stayed within the arm. "Great, you're sulking now, aren't you? Why is it I get a temperamental arm with an attitude problem?"


For the next hour as Alienbutt flew further into the unknown space claimed by the Wantooaninyougo priests he tried to get his arm talking again. The thought that he had gone totally mad began to cross his mind, so finally he gave up. He had to find the gateway and get home fast. The closer he got to the gateway, the more a feeling of foreboding was growing within him that he would be too late. His arm had destroyed two of the priesthood's ships and he knew nothing about them. Did he have a mighty fleet waiting for him or was this priesthood just a small bunch of nutters who liked to throw people into an abyss?

Suddenly an alarm went off on the flight desk and Alienbutt brought his ship to a stop while he checked the readout on the sensor computer screen. His sensor sweep had picked up an abnormality ahead of him that he didn't expect to find out here. Flicking to a visual view he began to magnify the space directly ahead of himself and there he saw proof to confirm the warning. At the edge of his viewing range a large fleet of ships sat frozen in time, marooned in dead space. Alienbutt sat back in his chair. The reason no ships ever came back from Wantooaninyougo space sat before him. Alienbutt had been taught by Ruck Bodgers how to find and navigate around the strange phenomenon while he had acted as a guide to Alienbutt on a bounty hunt. Now when Alienbutt flew, it had become second nature to set the scanners to include a dead space scan after seeing up close the consequence of getting trapped in it. Quickly Alienbutt sent out a dozen probes to get a wider view of what was before him. As they sent back data the computer converted it into a three dimensional holo-map, the area of dead space showing up purple. Alienbutt looked in shock at a wall of dead space, expanding as the probes sent back more information. Standing up he walked to the back of the flight cabin and grabbed a bottle of whiskey. With a curse he downed over half of it before looking back to the map. It was then something caught his eye.

"Computer, pan back on the image and then compute possible outcome of data."

Alienbutt watched as the computer decreased the size of the image and then filled in the most probable outcome of the data the probes were sending. Alienbutt walked back to his chair and sat down. Before him was a sphere of dead space over fifty million miles in diameter.

"Computer, I want the probes looking for any tunnels leading into the centre of that sphere. I'm gonna bet my bottom butt plug I need to get to the centre of that thing."

# CHAPTER 18

## Foolish Missions.

### INTERSTELLAR NEWS CHANNEL 9.
### NEWS FLASH.

News is coming in of an Ick raid on a trade convoy out of the planet Hardstool. The convoy, protected by two battle cruisers and carrying supplies for the Federation day celebrations was attacked and over ten thousand barrels of Hardstool whiskey was stolen. The attack was beaten off with minimum loss of life but the loss of the cargo has been brought up in the Senate, as part of the shipment was intended for the Senate's own celebrations. It is believed that the Ick had intended to disrupt coffee supplies from the planet Sloppystool and hit the wrong target. New supplies have been ordered but the price of Hardstool whiskey has doubled overnight.

Nifty and Blackarachnia were the last to arrive at the meeting. As they entered, the speaking stopped and both were instantly aware of tension in the room. Already seated at the table was Wickede, his arm bandaged, Snoodgrass and four Ick commanders. Admiral Frederick had already left to organise the Ick Fleet, ensuring everything would be ready. Hydroponic sat at the end of the table, a look of disgust on his face.

"Nifty, Blackarachnia, thank Sung you are here. Would you try to talk sense into your friend over there?" Wickede asked, glaring at Hydroponic, who glanced over at them and shrugged, dismissing the Ick leader's comments.

"With respect, Wickede, I am not Ick nor am I a bounty hunter now, despite Ramboe's tricks. You need more support and warriors. I think I can get them for you."

"You'll get yourself killed for nothing," Put in Snoodgrass as all the Ick rose to stand while Nifty took her seat at the table. Hydroponic sat and shook his head, bemused by their strange action as everyone sat back down.

"What's the plan, Hydro?" Blackarachnia asked, reaching out to pour a drink for Nifty and himself.

"You need more ships, I go and get them, it's simple," Hydroponic replied casually to his friend, leaning back in his chair.

"You've been back five minutes and found an army we all missed? I'm really impressed. Who is it?" Blackarachnia asked with a grin, before taking a sip of his drink.

"The Ji Hunters," stated Hydroponic in a bored voice. Blackarachnia nodded, his face not changing expression.

"Are we talking about the same Ji Hunters who kill anyone that enters their space? The Ji Hunters that last time the Federation sent a peace envoy to them, they raided the Chancellors home world and barbecued every animal and pet they found? We're talking about those Ji Hunters and not someone else going by the same name?"

"They're canny fighters though," replied Hydroponic with a grin.

Snoodgrass got to his feet, throwing his arms up in disgust. "I knew all those years alone would have affected your brain," he stormed. "Why do you think you can achieve what no one else has ever done and get the Ji on our side?"

Hydroponic sat forward, still grinning. "Because I know their secret magic word, the secret word that will get them to talk to me and join us in this war."

Snoodgrass stopped as all turned to stare at Hydroponic as he sat back again in his chair, looking smug.

"And what is this secret magic word, then?" Wickede asked, curious now.

"If I told you it wouldn't be secret, would it?" Pulling out a cigar he was about to light it when he saw the look on Nifty's face. "I'll just step outside and have this then, if that's OK. Give you lot a chance to talk about me."

Nifty gave a smile and a nod. "I think that would be best, Hydroponic. No point in stinking out this nice room, is there?" She turned to Blackarachnia and smiled. "With a little training he's not such a bad person, and his plan is really very good."

"I think you should explain what is going on, Nifty, before Snoodgrass explodes from not knowing everything that is happenin,." Wickede said. "You know what he's like where secrets that he doesn't know are involved."

Snoodgrass returned to his quarters. The meeting had dragged on as the planning for what was in all likelihood the final battle of the Ick Empire was discussed. They knew they were outnumbered and they would have to commit their entire forces in a desperate final gamble. Hydroponic's plan was madness. So was the Ick's, but at least Hydroponic's would only get himself killed. Unbuttoning his tunic he took it off and threw it onto the small bed, and then sat in the only seat in the small room. The worst part of the whole plan Wickede had saved until last. He had dropped a final bombshell and left Snoodgrass numb. Snoodgrass was to stay behind when the fleet set out and oversee the dispersal of all non-combatants to places of safety, in case the battle went badly. For a while Snoodgrass sat staring into space, lost in memories, running over all his plans, trying to find a mistake that would have made a difference. Suddenly he looked up with a start, seeing Blackarachnia standing at the door.

"It's hard to be left behind when you feel you're responsible for ensuring things go to plan," said the bounty hunter from the doorway. "If it's any consolation, with you to look after your people many more will survive, and me and Nifty will cover Wickede's back to the very end."

"You don't hold out hope then, Blackarachnia?"

"Never did, but I'll stand to the end."

"He's like a son to me. I brought him up since he had a snotty nose and thought a bottle should just hold milk," Snoodgrass said, his voice close to breaking.

"Well I've got some bottles that don't have milk in, so let's go find this son of yours and my wife and have a drink. We could even invite that fool Hydro."

"Just wish we could invite Alienbutt too," added Snoodgrass sadly.

"Me too, I would give everything I have to have him by our sides for this. He would have a way to make the plan seem less stupid," Blackarachnia said sadly.

"The Book says he will be there, do you not trust it?" Snoodgrass asked, standing up.

"The book seems to be going a bit wrong at the moment. When was the last time you had a prediction before an event happened, instead of reading about it afterwards?" Blackarachnia asked walking back through the door.

"Just before Alienbutt left to rescue Wickede," Snoodgrass said to himself.


General Jee walked into the small cell. On the wall opposite slumped the dead body of the prisoner, his bloody corpse held in place by electronic manacles. He turned to his chief torturer.

"Did you get the information needed before you let the priest die?"

"Yes General, we have all the codes we need to send a message to Snoodgrass as well as a list of his contacts. Would you like them to be picked up?"

"Not until the battle starts, I want nothing to endanger the trap we will spring. Have the message sent that the full Federation fleet will attack the Bounty Hunter space station in three weeks' time." General Jee turned to an officer standing in the doorway. "Have the fleet mobilised. We're going to end this war with one final battle. Send messages to the reserves to prepare. All droid ships are to be made ready to move on my order."

The officer saluted and left as Jee walked up to the dead man. "Snoodgrass may know of our build-up here and our current numbers, but when a million extra droid ships jump into the battle, the Ick and their allies will be swept away and into the pages of history."


Snoodgrass sat at the table in a stupor, not a big drinker. Wickede had been ensuring his glass had never been empty as they sat drinking and making toasts with Blackarachnia and Hydroponic, who had announced he would leave in the morning. Nifty already lay on the couch in the corner asleep.

Blackarachnia had placed a blanket over her and would not let his eyes stray from her sleeping form for more than a few moments. Suddenly Snoodgrass's ever-present electronic notebook began to beep. Drunkenly he picked it up and pressed the screen. As he read, his posture became more erect and the drunken look disappeared from his eyes.

"The Federation will attack the Bounty Hunter station within three weeks, seeking to split our forces. Then while they hold back the Fo'c'sle forces in Ashia Minor they will swing around and send their full force against us. They have been reinforced with five hundred thousand droid fighter units and carriers. With their battle cruisers and other fleet we're looking at odds of thirty to one on capital ships, even without the fighters added in." He looked around at the others who seemed to have sobered up too, apart from Hydroponic who grinned and lifted his glass.

"Here's to not having the most foolish mission anymore. I feel so much better for not being the daftest in the room."

Wickede grinned and lifted his glass also. "I'll meet you in the afterlife and see if you still think the same after your first meeting with the Ji." He stood up and pressed a button on the table. "Mr Rochester, order all fleet to battle stations. We leave in one hour." He turned to Snoodgrass. "Begin the evacuation. I want all our people out of here within the next thirty six hours."

Nifty sat up and yawned. "Alienbutt better hurry up and get back here soon then. I hope that fat-arsed fool doesn't turn up too late for this one."

Kali sat and read the message that had just arrived and looked over to Killashandra, passing her the message. "What fleet can be airborne within the hour?" she asked. Killashandra quickly looked at the message and shook her head.

"We can set off with sixty Fo'c'sle ships and maybe three hundred irregulars and other ships. If we message Grommit her unit can head straight to the station and that's another fifty. We have another couple of hundred ships almost ready that can fly and fight, but I don't rate their chances of coming back."

"I don't rate any of our chances of coming back. Order Cyborgpirate to withdraw all his forces back to the Bounty Hunter station. No point having a forward position, they'll be swarmed over when the Federation attack. Now let's order a red alert and start moving."

"And Prince Ponnfarr and his wife the Queen?"

"The Heeter squadron will come in useful. Outside the Fo'c'sle they're the best fighters we have. The Queen is proving to be a capable commander, when not thinking up ways to torture Ponnfarr and keep him on his toes. Send her a message and request her aid."

"You think she'll break off her attacks on the Federation based around Heeter?"

"Ponnfarr will convince her to join us. Despite what she says publicly she listens to his council, and if he wasn't so blind he would realise she's quite taken with him."

Killashandra grinned. "She is putting a lot of effort into training him. I just hope we have the time to see the finished product."

Kali looked down at the desk. "Ask the Queen if she will use her force to defend the production facilities when we pull our forces out. It gives them a chance of surviving and that's the best I can do."

Killashandra smiled. "Ponnfarr will know what you are doing."

"I know but his duty to protect the Queen will override his need to join us. He will know it is a lost cause," Kali said, meeting Killashandra's eye. "I always hoped we would win but we did damn well to last this long."

# CHAPTER 19

## Special Delivery for.

### INTERSTELLAR NEWS CHANNEL 9.
### NEWS FLASH.

The Senate today observed a minute's silence to mark the fourth anniversary of the outbreak of the War of the Coffee Bean. In a special address to the Federation Kraltic Vaspirlel, the leader of the Senate, called for continued support for the Federation forces as they bring about the final big push to bring the war to a victorious conclusion. He went on to give the thanks of the whole Senate and Federation to the Coffee Houses for their tireless work in delivering the cure for coffee addiction and its support for the armed forces. New legislation announced today named the Coffee Houses as Defenders of the Federation, and it is now a Federal Crime to act against their best interests. Senator Yashria, an opponent of the legislation, declared that this honour gave the Coffee Houses an unfair advantage in all business dealings as it is now a crime to be a business rival. He has become the first federation citizen arrested under the new law, and faces a minimum of life imprisonment.

Alienbutt brought his ship to a stop before the passage that led through the wall of dead space. He had tried sending probes into the tunnel, but the static discharge from dead space blanked out all information within the first couple of miles. He knew that he would have to fly into the sphere blind and hope a fleet of angry priests were not waiting for him in the centre. Alienbutt stood and walked to the back of the cabin and opened a large locker. Inside sat Frank's propulsion drive. Next to it were five large bottles full of a green gas that glowed. Pipes and wires connected each bottle to the drive. Flicking a switch, he closed the lid. The Ick ship, while small, was far more advanced than anything in this space, and for it to fall into anyone's hands would cause havoc to the status quo. After his run in with Quint he decided that he couldn't allow that to happen, so had worked on rigging up a self-destruct system. Using the limited items to hand he had come up with probably the largest yield on a bomb since the destruction of his home world. The five large bottles of refined Alienbutt essence, if used right, could have provided the energy to run a city for a decade. Just in case he wasn't around to active the self-destruction, he had come up with a foolproof back-up plan. Walking back to the flight desk he saw a large button had begun to flash red. Underneath it was a small sign saying; 'Emergency only. Do not press.'

Finally ready, he began to eat the two large kebabs he had placed on the co-pilots seat and grabbed the first of three bottles of whiskey. The ship began to move slowly forward as Alienbutt settled down to start the final leg of his journey home. Setting the sensor sweep to show on the viewe,r he flew down into the tunnel. Quickly he was surrounded by purple that showed the boundary of dead space all around him. The tunnel was over a mile across and stretched on as he travelled further into it. He kept the scanners on full, waiting for the first sign of an end to the tunnel. The weight of the surrounding dead space began to mentally crush down upon him and he began to increase speed, then slowly before him he saw the end of the tunnel appear. The black speck rapidly got larger as he approached the end of the tunnel, and then he was clear and into the centre of the sphere of dead space.

Alienbutt brought his ship to a stop. The space before him was enveloped in pitch blackness; not a shred of light managed to get through the surrounding bubble of dead space. Quickly, Alienbutt launched probes and sent out a number of flares, trying to see what was before him. The entire area was empty apart from a small barren planet. It measured about two thousand miles across. Any attempted scan was virtually useless, as the interference from the surrounding dead space distorted all but the basic information. Here on this lone planet, Alienbutt knew, was the location of the gateway that would lead him home and also the temple of the priests of Wantooaninyougo. Picking up no signs of life anywhere else within the area, Alienbutt headed towards the planet.

As he approached it Alienbutt scanned the planet's surface as best he could, searching for any signs of where the temple would be. After completing a wide orbit of the planet, he chose a site he thought most likely. The entire planet's surface was a rocky wasteland. In the area he chose to land, the signs of a large circular layout of what looked like ruined buildings stood, with what looked to be a giant pyramid in their centre. Other traces of what looked to be buildings had crumbled into the landscape, but here they looked better preserved. Buffeted by strong winds in the lower atmosphere, Alienbutt landed within walking distance of the central pyramid. Quickly he found the hostile environment suit, and placed his pistols into the holsters on the belt. Placing extra ammunition into the belt pouches he picked up the assault rifle and prepared to step out into the freezing atmosphere of the planet. Finally he placed the helmet on and tested the spotlight built into the top of it. Satisfied, he pressed the door release and then looked down at his metallic arm. "Well, I hope you're going to behave yourself this time."

Leaning into the wind, he began to walk across towards the pyramid that loomed over him. Its smooth sides towered into the sky, its peak lost in the swirling dust a mile above. Directly ahead was a dark doorway that he headed for, the only sign of an entrance. Reaching the opening he looked back to his ship, just visible through the dust-filled air.

Within a few steps the howling of the wind outside died down, the light on his helmet showing the way ahead down the cramped tunnel. The tunnel slopped downwards, the air getting warmer as he went along, with signs of moisture on the walls. Looking backwards along the way he had come, he saw only blackness and realised the tunnel was curved. From the display on his wrist-com he had descended over thirty feet when the tunnel opened out into a large chamber. The chamber was a large cavernous area, far wider than it was high. Strange beams of red and green lights lit up small areas, and smoke drifted around large square blocks towards the back. Alienbutt stood in the entrance carefully looking around, the light from his headlamp lighting up the darkness. As he finally walked into the hall, he saw a figure walk up between the strange square blocks. The red and green lights threw strange shadows, silhouetting him. The figure was dressed in a long robe and wearing a wide-brimmed hat. As Alienbutt watched, a further two figures also appeared through the smoke. Stopping his advance, Alienbutt went to bring his rifle to bear, but his robot arm refused to move. He tried to wiggle his fingers but to no avail. Looking back to where the figures stood, he saw more appearing through the smoke of other lights. Over twenty now stood unmoving in the billowing smoke, watching him, their eyes glowing red.

"So would any of you know the way to the temple of Wantooaninyougo?" Alienbutt asked, letting the rifle fall to the floor and placing his good hand on the handle of his holstered pistol. He didn't know what had gone wrong with his arm, but the timing couldn't have been worse.

"You seek the Exalted Grand Master, the anointed Wantooaninyougo, defender of the void?" a voice shouted in reply. "You have found him. Here is the last exit of those lost."

"If he's the boss, I'd like a quick word. Sounds like I'm in the wrong place," Alienbutt said, moving his hand to curl his fingers around the pistol's handle.

One of the figures stepped forward, his steps slow and deliberate. Alienbutt again tried to move the fingers of his robotic arm, but it still remained useless.

"I am the anointed Lucifus, High Priest of the ancient temple of Wantooaninyougo. We guide the lost to the last exit from this universe. If you are not lost, then state your reason for defiling our temple with your presence." The figure said, coming to stand before Alienbutt, his glowing eyes yellow. Alienbutt realised this was down to some sort of eyewear, partially hidden beneath his worn and scruffy looking hat. Looking closer, Alienbutt noticed the cloak was equally battered, the black colour partially covered in a strange white powder. The trousers and boots beneath were also covered in the same strange powder and made of some kind of leather that had been patched many times.

"You don't look much like a priest," Alienbutt observed.

"And you don't look like you stand any chance of drawing that weapon before my followers shoot you, so remove your hand," Lucifus replied with a chilling smile.

"I just seek passage to the gateway. Let me through and

no one gets hurt," Alienbutt said, looking past Lucifus to where the others stood half-hidden in the billowing smoke. Alienbutt felt movement behind him, but he responded too late as something struck him across the back of his helmet. Falling to his knees, the world began to spin as more blows rained down on him.

"You will get to see what you seek, but as for no one getting hurt, I can't promise that," Lucifus said quietly, bending down, then in a louder voice he announced: "We have an extra sacrifice, prepare the altar."

Alienbutt felt his arms dragged behind his back and restrained before being roughly dragged to his feet, his helmet ripped from his head. As he was being prepared to be taken away, a priest came rushing over.

"My Lord High Priest, another item has come through the void," he said breathlessly, holding out what looked like a bottle. "It hit Ebil on the back of the head as she was lighting the candles of perdition."

The High Priest looked at the item in the newcomer's hand. "Karaxeem, calm your excitement." He held out his hand and took the bottle, inspecting it. Alienbutt saw the bottle and grinned.

"Last chance Lucifus. You really don't want to get in my way," Alienbutt said, recognising the bottle of Hardstool single malt and knowing that beyond the gateway his friends waited.

Frank stood on the bridge of the science vessel. They were on the very edge of dead space. He watched through the viewing screen as a host of robots built a large platform in an area of space where the Stone of Bi used to be. The destruction of the stone had made their mission more difficult, but Frank had worked a way around the setback. He was having a giant eco bubble built that would allow them to begin their plan to let

Alienbutt know they were waiting for him. Using specialised scans that the stranger Fashion had told him about in his dream, he had pinpointed the area of space where the closed gateway was located. Now construction of what he needed was on the way. Snoodgrass had been sceptical of Frank's plan, but had assigned a science vessel and two dreadnoughts as escort, with a team of the best Outer System marines they had. The ever present robot Kirk walked onto the flight desk and toddled over to where Frank stood.

"It's time for the movie. The marines have requested The Thing from Outer Space. It's an excellent choice," Frank said in his monotone voice, but somehow he managed to indicate his excitement. The arrival of Major Kaela with his squad had been a minor miracle to Frank, as the marines loved to watch Kirk's films at every opportunity.

"I'm afraid I still have hours of programming to complete, Kirk, and those construction droids out there need watching to ensure they get the job done right. I simply cannot trust them like I do you," Frank said. He had discovered that Kirk had developed pride, and the best way to escape his film shows was to, as Wickede often said, blow smoke up his arse. "The platform should be ready tomorrow and I need to ensure everything is prepared," Frank continued. "I just hope the five hundred bottles of whiskey will be enough. It's all Snoodgrass could get hold of."

Kirk did a little hop that Frank knew meant he was shrugging his shoulders, and turned to leave. He knew the robot was upset, but while he had the marines to keep his film viewing tendencies occupied it gave Frank a much-needed breather.

Frank returned to thinking of the problem before him; sending bottles of Alienbutt's favourite whiskey through a closed gateway he now had to open. The other scientists on the bridge barely looked up as he began to mumble in binary code, as he considered how to solve the next little problem. He didn't bother to use the computer set aside for him when working, as it only slowed down his calculations.

# CHAPTER 20

## To Sacrifice an Alienbutt.

### INTERSTELLAR NEWS CHANNEL 9.
### NEWS FLASH.

As Federation Day approaches there have been calls for the easing of flight restrictions to allow families to meet up for the nine-yearly celebrations. With announcements that the Coffee Houses are expecting the largest crop of the bean in over ten years, many see Federation Day as a chance for celebration even in the present climate of rationing and restrictions. With the celebrations just days away, many planets are expected to announce the easing of planet-wide travel restrictions and martial law on many planets for the duration of the celebrations. It is thought that the restrictions on space travel will remain in force.

Alienbutt had been half dragged through the outer temple and thrown into a cell after being stripped. He now stood in just his battered leather kilt, the rest of his clothes removed. After hearing the heavy door to the holding area slam shut he looked around. Four large cells were within the stone room, but all stood empty. The bindings around his wrists had been removed so Alienbutt walked over to the bars and gave them an experimental shake but they held firm. It took a moment for him to realise that both his hands were working again. Stepping back he looked in fury at his robotic arm.

"What the bloody hell are you playing at? When I needed you to work you decide to play dead, but now we're locked up you're up for working again." For a second nothing happened and then the small screen popped up.

> YOU SET ME TO GENERAL USAGE AND
> THAT DOES NOT ALLOW REACTING TO
> POSSIBLE THREATS UNLESS HOST
> OVERRIDE IS ACTIVE.

"What do you mean unless host is active? I wanted you to be active, you stupid machine!" Alienbutt screamed in rage, smashing the arm into the cell bars.

> TEMPER TEMPER.
>
> I AM THE HOST, YOU ARE THE
> APPENDAGE, I THOUGHT YOU WOULD
> HAVE REALISED THAT.

"What sort of stupid bloody programming is that?" asked Alienbutt.

> IT IS ALL IN THE USER AGREEMENT.
> YOU DID READ IT BEFORE ACCEPTING,
> CYBERCORE IS NOT LIABLE FOR YOUR
> IGNORANCE IN OPERATING SYSTEMS.

"Of course I never read the agreement, I was unconscious having my arm chopped off at the time. I just woke up and you were there," Alienbutt said in disbelief.

CYBERCORE ISN'T LIABLE FOR
UNAUTHORISED FITTING OF ITS
HARDWARE.

Alienbutt looked up to the ceiling in despair. "The only thing liable will be me getting my heart cut out if you don't just start doing what I want you to do when I need you to do it. Do you have a program that covers that?"

HOW ABOUT TOTAL ANNIHILATION WITH
APPENDAGE OVERRIDE. I GET TO KILL
BUT NEED PERMISSION FOR UNARMED
TARGETS.

Alienbutt looked over towards the door and his pile of clothes and his boots. "That will have to do for now. First thing we need to do is get out of this cage and get my boots and butt plugs back. Then we need some weapons," Alienbutt said, looking at the lock on the cage door. Suddenly a flap slid back on his metal forearm and a small grenade launcher rose up to sit flush.

"No shooting that thing yet, I've a quieter way to open the lock," Alienbutt said, putting his hand over the grenade launcher. With that Alienbutt turned around and bent over. Careful aim wasn't needed as the blast radius melted a foot-wide area of the bars around the lock. Pushing open the door, Alienbutt walked over to retrieve his belongings. Everything was there, apart from his weapons and the amulet.

IF YOU HAVE THAT INBUILT WEAPON,
WHY DO YOU NEED ME?

Alienbutt looked at the screen and the melted lock. "I've

got a bit of a dodgy tummy, my gas isn't building right so I need to conserve the bit I have."

The Temple of Wantooaninyougo had existed for thousands of years, the last defenders of the void. The priests and priestesses were all of the people, the last descendants of a once great civilisation. Only a fraction of their ancient knowledge had survived the passage of time, just like the people themselves. The civilisation that had travelled the stars and crossed dimensions was now reduced to a dead rock of a planet, all but trapped within a bubble of dead space. Over a thousand years ago the High Priest had discovered how to use the ancient powder that prevented them dying of old age, their bodies held locked in time in the same way that the dead space trapped the ships all around them. But with the passing years the dead space had spread, so now only a tiny passage remained. The High Priest insisted that the sacrifice of people into the void would reverse the spread of dead space but Ebil Kitty, the last priestess at the temple, knew the High Priest was mad and would say anything. The fact that he was mad didn't bother her, as the voices in her head had confided that she too was at the wrong side of bonkers to pass judgement. She looked up as Karaxeem walked into the void room with an arm full of candles, ready to set up the altar for tonight's sacrifice. He looked nervously at the grey disc of the void that hung in the air behind the altar, a shimmering oval some twenty feet across. The sudden appearance of the bottles flying out of it had terrified Karaxeem, as the first one had hit him full in the face. Since then a further fifty plus had arrived, the first ones smashing on the stone floor, but now great cushions littered the inner sanctum's floor to avoid the breakages of the void's bounty. Still they did not know what they were, and the High Priest had not told them what it could mean. With the arrival of the stranger who had destroyed two of their remaining four ships, most of the priests were on edge as to what was going on. It wasn't unheard of for things to come through the void, but never had they come through so regularly. Ebil Kitty remembered the strange man who had come through carrying the holy badge of the Priests. Lucifus was convinced he was sent to aid them, but the first chance he got he had flown off in one of their ships. Now this stranger returned carrying the same badge. Karaxeem began to put out the candles, replacing those used in the last sacrifice for fresh ones, nervously casting glances towards the void. Still, he missed seeing a fresh bottle enter and Ebil Kitty watched as it flew across the room to bounce off the back of his head. Karaxeem fell without a sound. Ebil Kitty stood and watched the ripples on the void, and just for a moment she thought she saw a metal face with a single round eye. From far off she heard strange words in a monotonous voice.

"I'm sure I just hit someone with that bottle, Frank."

Alienbutt opened the door slightly and peered through. The corridor was empty. Swiftly he began to walk down it, his metallic arm held out before him, the grenade launcher ready to be fired at his spoken command. He was halfway down the corridor when the door at the far end opened and a group of priests walked through. The first stopped as he saw Alienbutt, and the ones behind him walked into him. Before anyone could react the grenade launcher on Alienbutt's arm fired. The small grenade hit the priest in the chest and exploded. The force of the blast in the tunnel knocked Alienbutt off his feet. Coughing he got to his knees. The tunnel was full of smoke, dust and sticky wet bits of priest.

"What are you doing? You were supposed to wait for my command!" Alienbutt screamed. He looked to the small screen.

```
SORRY, FINGER SLIPPED.
```

"You don't have fingers. What did I tell you about killing unarmed people?" Alienbutt,replied, getting back to his feet

```
THEY ALL HAD TWO ARMS, I CHECKED
FIRST.
```

Lucifus stood waiting in the outer sanctum, his executioner Skatos beside him, while the priests knelt in rows before him waiting for the sermon to begin. All waited for the sacrifice to be brought in. This sermon would be different, for Lucifus wore the stranger's amulet. The void's secrets would be revealed to him with this sacrifice and the priests would enter a new dawn for their order. Ebil Kitty and Karaxeem, his head bandaged, stood off to one side, controlling the red and green lighting and smoke jets that set the atmosphere for the proceedings; Lucifus liked to have dramatic effects for when he spoke to the faithful. When the explosion rocked the temple all looked at each other, their fear evident, then as one all gazes fell upon the High Priest Lucifus and the crazed expression on his face.

"As the day we have worked towards approaches, we are being tested," he began. "Only those worthy will go forth from here to rule the universe. You must take up your faith and wear it as a shield to protect you." His voice began to rise to a scream. "Take up your holy weapons and bring me the unclean heretic's body."

The priests stood up in silence and turned to leave. Lucifus indicated that Skatos should remain with him. Once the room was empty Lucifus turned and entered the inner sanctum, Skatos a step behind. Ebil Kitty looked around at the empty sanctum and had the first clear and sane thought for over five hundred years. She grabbed Karaxeem by the arm and stood up, dragging him with her.

"Come on," she said, heading for a side door.

"Where are we going?" Karaxeem asked, still suffering a concussion from the blow to the head by the flying whiskey bottle.

"The stranger's ship. You wanna know why I'm the last priestess alive?" she said, going through the doorway.

"Because you didn't die?" Karaxeem asked innocently. Ebil Kitty let the comment go. Karaxeem might look like someone in their mid-years but he was the oldest of them, and the youth powder couldn't fully stop the mind losing its sharpness, and it had been fairly blunt to start with. She was still alive because she had always known when to fight and when to make herself scarce. Something about this stranger told her to make herself scarce.

Alienbutt bent down next to the body of one of the priests and removed the circular goggles that he wore. Placing them over his eyes, he looked around the dark smoky temple, the air made even thicker by the explosions from his arm-mounted grenade launcher that had decimated the attacking priests. The goggles worked to make things even darker, so Alienbutt pushed them up onto his forehead and picked up the priest's elaborate pistol. Pointing the gun at the wall he pulled the trigger, and a disappointingly small bullet shot out to make a small chip in the stonework. Turning back around he just had time to register a figure standing before him, its eyes glowing red beneath its wide brimmed hat, before it hit him on the side of the head with a large staff.

Other priests ran out of hiding to surround Alienbutt as he lay unconscious. Two set about smashing the metallic arm with their heavy staffs until sparks and smoke began to rise. Only then did they lift up his feet and begin to drag him off.

Alienbutt awoke to a sharp pain in the side of his head and a feeling of being stretched. Opening his eyes, he quickly looked around a darkened room. His gaze was drawn to a large grey oval that floated off to his left. The room was full of dark shadows and smoke billowed all around. A strange rhythmic drumming sound filled the air with an ancient tribal quality. Alienbutt was lying on his back on some sort of table, spreadeagled. He tried to sit up, then realised he was chained down by the ankles and wrist. Looking over to his robotic arm he saw it was smashed below the elbow, metal rods and wires hanging loose. Hearing a noise he looked over to see dark shadows moving through the smoke towards him. Most stopped so they remained hazy shadows, but two approached, both dressed in full length black robes with their hoods up to hide their faces. Alienbutt's eyes were drawn to the second figure and the large serrated knife that he held in one hand. The one holding the knife took up position standing at Alienbutt's head while the other went and stood at his feet.

"For the defilement you have caused within the hallowed walls of our temple and the murder of our brothers, your suffering will be terrible," the one at his feet said, and Alienbutt realised that it was the High Priest Lucifus. "You will suffer the sermon of a thousand cuts; the skin of your chest will be flayed from your living body. Each piece will be fed to the void. Skatos the executioner has had a thousand years to perfect his art. Your suffering will become legend. It will release us from the orb of dead space and free the spirit of the void into our bodies, and the universe will bow to us as we become its new gods."

Skatos held his arms out, the knife in both hands and slowly brought it down to puncture the skin on Alienbutt's chest. As Alienbutt gritted his teeth against the pain, Lucifus screamed out in joy.

"Look, the void reacts to our sacrifice!"

All eyes turned to stare at the void as it began to ripple, and then a bottle flew out of it to hit Skatos on the side of the head. He collapsed, the knife falling from his fingers. Alienbutt took advantage of the momentary stunned silence, and arching his back he lifted his butt cheeks off the altar stone he was chained to. With a slight twist and internal push all four butt plugs flew from their nesting place in an explosion of Alienbutt essence. Lucifus never discovered what hit him as the butt plugs ripped through his body, closely followed by the engulfing gas cloud. Within seconds Alienbutt heard choking noises, quickly followed by the sound of people falling over.

In the silence that followed Alienbutt pulled on the chain holding his arm in place, but it was securely fastened. Then a light began to blink on his wrist-com.

"Oh shit, not now." Alienbutt began to pull desperately at the chains in panic.

Ebil Kitty and Karaxeem quickly reached the stranger's ship and after a short while she had opened the door. Entering the cramped ship, she looked around.

"Karaxeem, go sit in the left hand chair and don't touch anything, while I close the door and check what stores there are on board."

She quickly closed the door and then stood inspecting the strange computer consoles and screens at the back of the ship. Shrugging her shoulders, she went up to the front of the ship and took the other seat. In front of Karaxeem was a large red flashing button with a strange sign underneath it. By the button was a screen, with what appeared to be numbers counting down.

"Did you press that button, Karaxeem?" she asked in dread.

"I may have caught it accidentally, but I didn't press it press it but it is flashing faster since I didn't press it," he replied sheepishly. "Is that countdown screen bad, do you think?"

"I think we have lived long lives and we will soon meet what is beyond the void," Ebil Kitty said with a slight smile.

"Are we going to ascend into the void like Lucifus promised, then?" Karaxeem asked hopefully.

"Well, we'll soon know the answer," she replied, watching the screen.

Alienbutt thrashed and screamed in rage against the chains but to no avail. Someone had pressed the self-destruct button on his ship, and he had five minutes to get free, and the only other people on this rock of a planet would not be waking up for a good twelve hours.

# CHAPTER 21

## Fluffy's Big Plan.

### INTERSTELLAR NEWS CHANNEL 9.
### NEWS FLASH.

The Senate today announced that martial law will be lifted on all but the most unstable planets for a week-long celebration to mark Federation day. With rumours of the war being almost won hopes of a return to normal life are high. The coffee bean drought has officially been declared over after the best harvest in over ten years, combined with the cure for coffee addiction. The combined good news is set to make these celebrations the biggest in living memory and many are already heralding the start of a new age of peace starting with the nine-yearly celebrations. The fact that the Senate elections that herald the start of Federation day have not gone ahead is not affecting the mounting excitement.

Mr Fluffy sat in his control room watching the giant holo-screen that beamed pictures from the nano camera implanted in Geurick's eye. His ship was hidden, watching the Ick fleet departing to go to the aid of the bounty hunters. The journey would take them two days and marked the start of his master plan. Already the Federation fleet was massing and ready to launch. Soon he would be the only power left in the universe, as he pulled the strings that would destroy both prophecies and leave the entire universe in chaos. The Federation had taken delivery of the last of his reprogrammed droid ships and battle units a week ago, and with the official order to suspend production to conserve resources, Mr Fluffy had begun work on a new project. He changed the image on the giant holo-screen with a thought. His brain was uplinked to his battle suit and then linked into the control room's entire system. He acted as a living central computer, controlling everything. The image came into focus of a giant new ship that was being built. It would be the most advanced and largest ship ever built. Mr Fluffy had spent his time waiting designing the ship, and now was free to build it. Within its giant cargo bay you would be able to park four of the Federation battle cruisers. The engines that powered the ship would work on his own concept of a solar drain warp drive. He would drain the very energy from whichever sun he felt like to power the ship, and with hundreds of thousands of suns to choose from, he could turn as many of the universe's lights off as he wished, so energy refills would not be a problem. After watching the thousands of robots swarming over the construction for a minute Mr Fluffy began to get bored, so popped the hatch on his battle suit, and with a thought, disconnected the upload link from the back of his skull. Nimbly he jumped out. Stretching his feline body he waited as one of the mind controlled scientists walked over to him and removed the nappy he had to wear inside the battle suit. Walking over to one of the cabinets that held the control units for the construction plants, he sprayed up the metal casing, before jumping up to settle down on a cushion next to a small heater vent and going to sleep.

Waking up as a tin of fish was opened, Mr Fluffy jumped down and started to wash himself. He had slept and dozed for almost twelve hours and knew the Ick fleet would be well on its way, while the forces from the Ashia Minor system would be close to the Bounty Hunter space station. Soon the Federation forces would begin their attack and as soon as battle was joined he would act. A human scientist placed a golden bowl on the floor beside him and Mr Fluffy turned his attention to eating, which would be followed by time spent chasing a wind-up mouse around the control room. After all, despite his massive intellect he was still a cat, and the wind-up mouse was great fun.

Hydroponic ran over his plan. He had kept it simple and not gone overboard on planning: enter Ji space and when they approached him, say the secret word to ensure he wouldn't get blown up. Then it was simple, convince them to join forces with the Ick and set off to the battle. He had not considered the fact that the violent little bleeders would come aboard his ship and while still grinning and accepting the drinks he offered, kick the crap out of him before gagging and binding him.

Now he sat in a small dark cell, one eye swollen shut and at least two ribs cracked, waiting to see what they would do next. A door opened down the corridor and he heard someone walk down and stop outside the cell. A small section of the door was slid back and light flooded in, blinding him and making his eyes water.

"Wat tha doin ere big un an ow yer no ar word?" A voice

asked through the door. Hydroponic considered a number of answers about alliances and the war, but dismissed them. He hated the fact that somewhere Snoodgrass would be sitting back, saying "I told you so." Instead he went for the right response and ensured he lived a bit longer.

"Where's my bloody room service, and when was the last time you cleaned up in here, you bunch of filthy little sods? You'd better get the boss down here as I'm starting to get pissed off with all this, and I'll not tell you about the great pet hunt that's about to start. Do you really want to miss hunting the cat?" Hydroponic sat back and waited for the effect of his outburst. From beyond the door he heard urgent conversation and then cheering. After a couple of minutes the excitement died down and then the ji that had spoken to him started giving orders.

"Get the big un out n tek im up to hall so we can chat n av a scoff, I wanna know abart this ere pet hunt."

Mr Fluffy was back within his battle suit, watching the large timer on countdown. Already the first elements of the Federation fleets had engaged the outer elements of Duke Ramboe's defences, smashing through them with sheer weight of numbers. The Ick fleet was less than four hours away, while the Fo'c'sle had already arrived. All was in place and it was time for him to act. Purring loudly he walked over and flicked a large switch on the control terminal. He could have started the act with a thought but as he was about to start taking over the universe, he felt it only proper to do it manually. A small panel slid back on the control panel and revealed a large red illuminated button, Purring even louder, Mr Fluffy pressed the button. Nothing seemed to happen, no sound or flashing lights. The activity within the room continued as before, but across the universe a series of events began to happen.

The Grand Master of the assassin's guild sat watching the celebrations in advance of Federation Day the following morning. Across the entire Federation, on every planet the peoples would be starting to celebrate, apart from those who were in the Federation Navy, who even now were beginning the offensive to end the war. They thought they were giving their lives to ensure the Federation survived, when in fact they were fighting for the Secret Order of the Coffee Bean and its plan to take over not just the Federation, but the entire universe.

Taking another sip of coffee he sat back to enjoy the pictures of the happy masses on the screen before him, when one of the novices knocked on the door and walked in.

"Excuse me, Grand Master, but the security computer is picking up some strange readings from Geurick's apartment," the novice said nervously. Angered by the interruption the Grand Master stood up and turned to face the novice.

"Define strange, boy, an assassin always needs to act with all the facts or he is a dead assassin. Now is not a time to forget your training."

"The computer is unable to get a fix on what is happening in the rooms. There is massive temperature fluctuation and magnetic surges, and it seems to be getting more intense."

The Grand Master started to walk towards the door when the building was hit by what seemed to be an earthquake. He stumbled into a wall as great cracks appeared up the walls. The question he started to ask was never finished as a further, even greater earthquake hit and the planet's molten core erupted upwards as the planet started to turn itself inside out.

A hundred thousand miles out from the capital planet of the Federation, a small transport ship carrying one million barbecue rack of ribs for the Federal Senate's grand banquet watched in horrified amazement as the planet imploded before them. Finally the trader who owned the cargo spoke to the ship's captain.

"Was it something you did?"

"I'm not hanging around to find out. The shit's gonna hit the fan really soon and I want to be a long way away when it does," replied the Captain, already punching a new course into the ship's computer.

"But what about my cargo?" the trader asked in a quivering voice.

"I just hope you got payment up front as the Senate won't be needing them now."

The last of the refugees' ships had been dispatched. Within an hour Wickede and the Ick Fleet would jump out of light speed and join the battle that already raged as the Federation tried to overwhelm Duke Ramboe's forces. Snoodgrass had headed back to his quarters, hoping to have half an hour's peace. He had been on the go for two days as he organised the dispersal of his people. As soon as he entered the room his communicator came to life.

"Commander Snoodgrass, there's a problem with the Ick navigation systems. We're getting reports from the refugee ships that all are experiencing a massive deviation and are locked out of manual controls."

"What of the fleet?" asked Snoodgrass, suddenly all thoughts of rest gone. If the fleet's navigation suffered the same problem travelling at light speed, the consequences could be disastrous. Snoodgrass felt more than heard movement behind him, and spun around to be confronted with a tall figure dressed in black. A small pistol was aimed at him. He knew instantly that he faced an assassin from the Coffee Houses, and knew which one it would be.

"Geurick Tackful, I presume," he said, knowing that there was nothing he could do to prevent what was about to happen. The figure nodded before firing once knocking the Ick commander off his feet. Snoodgrass felt no pain as he slumped to the floor and looking down saw a spreading red stain on his chest. Geurick walked over to stand above him and aimed the pistol again.

"Wickede and your fleet are doomed. There was nothing you could have done to save them." He fired a second time before turning and walking out of the room, leaving the body of the dead Ick commander. As he left, he heard the voice over the intercom sounding panicked.

"Commander Snoodgrass, the fleet has veered off course and is accelerating. It's heading straight towards dead space, and the monks of Ick have gone crazy. They say the Book is empty."

A security team burst into Snoodgrass's room a minute later. They had just enough time to inform central control room that the Ick commander had been assassinated before an explosion ripped apart the Ick control centre.

# CHAPTER 22

## The Battle of Hunters Rest.

### INTERSTELLAR NEWS CHANNEL 9.
### NEWS FLASH.

Large earthquakes and magnetic fluctuations have been reported on Capital planet just before contact was lost. Pictures from a live stream from the Senate sub-committee on domestic robot rights clearly show what appears to be a large scale earthquake. All contact with our office on Capital planet has been lost and as yet security forces have not commented on what has occurred there.

In more breaking news on the eve of Federation day a number of Federation Battle droids outside our studios seem to have malfunctioned and security forces are, as we speak, involved in a fire fight with them. Large explosions have been heard and a number of injured security staff were dragged into the lobby before lockdown procedures sealed our building. Unconfirmed reports from outside suggest a massacre of civilians by the heavily armoured battle droids that are still at large within the city.

It appears we have a breach in our studios and the evacuation signal has sounded.... The battle droids are inside the studio, we are under attack.

The fleet under the command of Commander Kali had arrived just as the main Federation fleet had engaged. Jumping out of light speed at the edge of the system where the bounty hunters' station was, situated she took a minute to take in the scene before her.

"This is Kali to fleet, we need to take out the battle cruisers before they can target the station. Killashandra, take your ships and hit the command vessels, the rest of you follow me. Alienbutt attack; run, hit and run," she ordered, using the attack plan devised by Alienbutt and Grommit before the battle of Dagnabbit. As Kali's ships began their attack run, Cyborgpirate and his ships fell into formation with them. The surviving members of the Fo'c'sle squadron attacked as one. Thousands of droid fighters rushed out to intercept them as they approached their target. The forward guns of the Fo'c'sle fleet opened fire and the front ranks of the fighters disappeared in a ripple of explosions, but more followed and by sheer numbers they were soon engulfed by a wave of defending fighters. Still the droids depended on numbers more than their weapon strength to try and stop their advance towards the battle cruisers. Losses would be inevitable, but they quickly burst through the fighters and launched a wave of torpedoes at the battle cruisers before peeling off as the battle cruisers began to return fire.

Kali ordered her ships to re-form and prepare for another attack. She was taking heavy losses, even though they were inflicting massive damage on the federation battle cruisers. The sheer numbers of enemy ships made the damage they were causing ineffective in the long term.

Killashandra rose high above the battlefield, her squadron following. From the advantage point she quickly viewed the scene of carnage below. The giant space station was taking colossal fire but so far the shields were holding up and the defending fleet were preventing any Federation ship getting close to it. At the back of the Federation fleet, behind the mass of battle cruisers, a large control ship lurked.

"Comander Killashandra, a number of Federation frigates are moving to intercept us," her security officer informed her. "They'll be within range in less than a minute."

Killashandra looked at the viewing screen, where over fifty enemy ships had broken away from the main battle to engage her squadron. With a grin she opened communication to her ships.

"Let's convince those frigates they didn't bring enough friends, then a full speed attack run on that command vessel. I want to see it burning after the first sweep, as I hate to repeat myself," she ordered, and as one the fifteen ships of her command turned to swoop down at the advancing Federation ships.

General Jee looked on in satisfaction as explosions began to rip through the giant space station. The battle was still fierce, but the loss of the station would be the turning point. The Ick fleet worried him as it was overdue, but they would not be able to turn the tide of this battle with the loss of the space station. He knew that somewhere out there his sister would be fighting for her life or even already dead, and it still rankled him that he would not see her die first-hand.

"General, we have a message from the reserve fleets. Commander Servios reports they are under attack."

Jee spun around to face his communications officer. "The Ick?" he asked, shocked that they had managed to outflank them and find the reserve force.

"No sir, it appears the droid units have..." he paused, unsure of how to say what was happening. Finally he found the word, "...mutinied, Sir. The droids are attacking and destroying the rest of our fleet."

Jee staggered backwards not understanding what he was hearing. How could droids change sides?

"Sir, we are getting reports from all over the battlefield now of the same thing, the droids are now attacking both sides." The communications officer looked worriedly over at the door as gunfire was heard outside the bridge doors. Seventy per cent of the Federation fleet was now made up of droid units.

"General," he pushed on. "We have lost contact with the reserves, but sensors show they are all moving up in attack formation. They will be here in under ten minutes." Further rounds of gunfire and explosions began to be heard from within the ship. The security officer cleared his throat and Jee switched his attention to him.

"We have reports of rogue droids on most decks Sir, we are taking losses, but hope to regain full control soon."

Jee smashed his fist down onto the console and turned to the tactical officer.

"Order all fleet to switch targets to the droid units, and try to open communications with the rebels advising them that a million fresh robot units are heading this way. Ask for a temporary alliance, or we are all dead."

Turning finally to the ship's pilot he continued. "Plot us a course out of here and be ready to move on my order. Once those reserves get here, anyone who is still here will be destroyed. Order all ships that are able, to prepare to retreat. I want us out of here with as many ships as possible. This battle is lost, but I intend to find out who the hell has betrayed me."

Duke Ramboe stood on the bridge of the space station watching the battle unfold. The men and women on the bridge went about their tasks with a quiet efficiency that was in total opposition to the battle that raged all around them.

As the shields were starting to fail, airlocks were sealed ready for when the explosions would begin to tear holes in the structure. The mission he had given them was to keep the station's weapons firing for as long as possible. All personnel not needed to directly aid the defence of the Hunters Rest had been evacuated. The only people left aboard were those in this room, and volunteers manning the hundreds of gun turrets. All aboard knew that to stay aboard was a death sentence, as the Federation would crash against the station with their full might to destroy it. A large explosion shook the station and Duke Ramboe looked down at the screen before him that showed a layout of the station. The shields in sector twelve had failed and now the area had become the main target for the battle cruisers, ripping holes in the station.

"Orders to Commander Grommit. She is to prepare to take charge of defences. If the Ick have not arrived when the station falls, she starts the withdrawal," Duke Ramboe ordered. The message was quickly sent as more explosions shook the station. Then the expected onslaught by the Federation battle cruisers failed to happen. Instead the attack seemed to pause, and Duke Ramboe watched in disbelief as the droid units began to attack their own ships.

"Someone find out what the hell is happening?" Duke Ramboe demanded. "Order all fleet to regroup while we have a chance."

"General, we're being hailed by the Federation command ship," the communication officer announced, sounding confused. "They're asking for a ceasefire. They are advising us that a million extra droid units are closing in and..." she paused. "Sir, the droids have gone rogue, they're attacking both sides."

Duke Ramboe stood, his mind racing as he watched the attacking Federation fleet as it self-destructed, ships exploding with no sign of incoming fire. The droid ships swarmed around the battlefield, attacking both sides.

"Orders to all fleet, switch targets, droid ships to be targeted only! I want long range scans for that incoming fleet," Duke Ramboe ordered. "All damaged ships to prepare for immediate evacuation on my order."

Kali heard Duke Ramboe's orders with disbelief. Before her she could see the heart of the Federation fleet being ripped apart.

"We have our orders, droid ships only and keep an eye out for that new fleet. I want all Fo'c'sle ships on me," she ordered. The remaining Fo'c'sle ships moved into position behind their leader's ship just as the droid armada arrived. With little time to react the Fo'c'sle turned to meet the threat head on as it swarmed over the rear of the Federation fleet and rolled on towards them. Thousands of large droid carriers spewed out hundreds of thousands of droid fighter ships, while tens of thousands of droid frigate class ships opened fire with their large forward cannons. The Federation had created a fleet of capital ships needing no living crews, controlled by a computer and manned by droids. In its first battle it had turned on its owners, and now everyone would fall before it.

Killashandra led the remains of her squadron toward Kali when the droid ships arrived, and watched in horror as the Fo'c'sle were swarmed over. Banking her ship away from the arriving fleet she knew there was only one thing they could do even before Duke Ramboe gave the order for a full retreat. The numbers and momentum of the droid charge through the battlefield was unstoppable.

"Killashandra to all ships, you heard the order, let's get above this mayhem, and then we run for it." As her pilot started to pull the ship clear of the battle she cast a last look at the Hunters Rest as the first of the droid ships reached it, its gun turrets causing massive damage but unable to stem the tide. As her ship picked up speed to pull away from the battlefield, droid ships closed in on them and opened fire. She knew it would be a close run race for them to escape.

# CHAPTER 23

## Aftermath.

### Teachings of Sung, the One Eyed Lama.

"When you stand on the top of a mountain and look down on the world, anything is possible. It is only when you surround yourself with people who tell you nothing is possible that you fail. We must all strive to stay on top of the mountain."

The teachings of Sung the One-eyed Lama.

This led to millions of people freezing to death or being thrown from their position at the summit of mountains as followers fought to stand at the very top.

Despite the fact that the Ji Hunters were technologically advanced, having stolen equipment from just about every race known, they lived a simple life. Their main food of choice was spit-roast animals and vegetables, although the vegetables were just there to throw at whatever target caught their eye while they ate. Convincing them to go to war had been easy, Hydroponic decided, as he picked at a rack of spare ribs. He had told the story of finding one of their ships adrift and told of the Captain's word about the great pet hunt. The response had been instant; the entire hall full of at least ten thousand feasting Ji had roared and screamed for war and revenge. The Big Ji had raised an animal horn to his lips and blown a powerful note that was taken up by others as they also grabbed their horns. It seemed the Ji were ready to go to war. Now the trouble was getting them to stop celebrating the fact that they were at war, and persuading them to actually get in their ships and set off to fight. For a day they had drunk themselves into a stupor, so he was surprised when their leader, known as Big Ji, walked up to Hydroponic, looking sober.

"I got sum news fo ya, an it aint gud, we bin listenin into that big scrap goin on over at Duke Ramboe's place and sum skunner as hijacked ya war an is wipin out both sides. Yud betta ave a look at t'news we is getting."

Blackarachnia's ship jumped out of light speed and came to a stop as it waited for the rest of the Ick fleet. Nifty sat at the pilot's chair while Blackarachnia sat ready at the weapons controls. The ship borrowed from Duke Ramboe was faster than anything the Ick had, so after a couple of minutes waiting, Blackarachnia finally spoke.

"Was you speeding to get here, Nifty?"

"Of course not, why do you think it's my fault? If anything I bet you gave me the wrong co-ordinates. You landed us in the wrong place," she said defensively.

"It wasn't me, I sent you the directions straight from the satellite navigation system." He turned on the communication and started flicking through channels.

"Well I bet Ramboe put a cheap sat-nav in then. I keep telling you, you can't trust them sat-navs, they're always sending you the wrong way. It only takes a bit longer to work the route out yourself, but no, you're too lazy," Nifty replied with an edge to her voice that Blackarachnia knew if he said the wrong thing, would lead to an argument he would never win. He chose to sidestep the issue and report on what he did know.

"Nothing on the Ick channel, but a lot of chatter from the Hunters Rest. Something real strange is going on, Nifty. Ramboe has just ordered a ceasefire with the Federation; they are just to target droid ships." He looked over, confused. "He's ordering a full retreat."

"Where the hell is Wickede and the Ick? Try to get hold of Ramboe," Nifty said, starting to power up the ship. "We need to know what's happening."

Blackarachnia flicked the radio onto speaker and sent out a message to the Bounty Hunter commander. After a moment he responded.

"Blackarachnia, where the hell are the Ick? It's all gone mad here. The droid ships have turned on everyone. We're trying to cover the fleet's retreat from the station, but our shields are buckling. We have..."

The radio went silent and Nifty and Blackarachnia looked at each other, before Nifty jumped up.

"I need to see the Book," she shouted as she rushed off to their quarters. Blackarachnia flicked to the secure Ick channel as he sought to pick up a transmission from Ick command.

Nifty raced into their room and grabbed the Book of Ick

that sat on a small table next to the bed. Opening a page at random she stared in disbelief at the blank page. Flicking through, she saw each page was the same. Not one word of prophecy remained in the entire book. Finally she returned to the first page and as she sat looking at the blank page, two words appeared.

## NEED ALIENBUTT.

She didn't hear Blackarachnia enter behind her. It wasn't until he placed his hand on her shoulder that she looked up at him. The look on his face filled her with dread.

"I've just intercepted an Ick transmission. The Ick are not coming. The entire fleet flew into dead space, some sort of navigation error. No one knows how or what happened, and..." he paused and took a deep breath. "Snoodgrass is dead. He's been assassinated, and the central command at Dagnabbit has been destroyed."

Killashandra sat in her ship's office, trying to make sense of what had happened. She had managed to escape the battle with what was left of her squadron. The squadron was now just six ships, and two of those so badly damaged they would have to be left, once all crew and usable equipment had been removed. They hid within the asteroid fields of Ashia Minor, hoping to make contact with other survivors, but all usual channels of communication were down. Even the secure Ick frequencies were full of interference.

Killashandra remembered the events of the battle. The Fo'c'sle and allies had arrived to bolster the bounty hunters and when the Federation attacked, the sheer numbers had almost overwhelmed the defenders. The battle had swayed as the greater skill of the defenders made up for the lack of numbers and the defenders knew that the Ick fleet would arrive soon. The Federation had learnt lessons from the battle of Dagnabbit and kept their battle cruisers back from the main battle where their massive fire power could be better used. Instead they sent forward their droid fighters and small frigates to swarm the defences. The Fo'c'sle again used their skill and speed to launch lightning raids into the battle cruisers, inflicting great damage. Without the Ick all knew the battle would be lost, and as the shield for the great space station began to fail under the continuous firepower of the Federation forces, the battle suddenly changed.

Killashandra still couldn't understand what had happened, but as one the droid ships had started firing upon the Federation ships, many swinging around and swarming back towards the battle cruisers. It descended into a three way battle, and then the Federation sent messages asking for a temporary alliance so that the droids could be destroyed. All federation ships ceased their attacks upon them and turned their attention to the droids. The problem for the Federation was that many of their ships had droids within them and they began to explode, destroyed from within. Then a second droid fleet arrived, swarming over the battle, their numbers uncountable and Duke Ramboe gave out the order for a full retreat. Killashandra had ordered all her squadron to follow her and just before they had gotten clear of the battle to jump to light speed, she had seen the giant space station being engulfed in explosions. The battle was lost to both sides, and the carnage was terrible beyond belief. As her pilot flew for their lives, she had a chance to view the battlefield. Other ships were also trying to get clear but the droids were destroying them before they got the chance. One of her squadron flying alongside them had taken a direct hit and, losing control, had swerved towards their ship. Only the reactions of her pilot had saved them. Another ship behind had not been so lucky, and both disappeared in a giant explosion. Finally they were clear and they managed the jump to safety.

The bounty hunter Captain Nobel walked into Killashandra's office. During the war they had become close friends as they had worked together, responsible for protecting the giant resource mines of Ashia Minor. Nobel took a seat across from Killashandra and winced as she sat, the wounds she had taken a few months ago still causing her pain.

"We just managed to get hold of a partial message from the Ick high command," she said to Kilashandra. Her face was drained of colour and her voice quiet. Killashandra cocked her head, waiting for Noble to continue. "The entire Ick fleet is gone. We couldn't work out the details from the message."

Killashandra's face drained of colour at what she had been told. "Then all is lost," she said in a near whisper.

"It gets worse. Snoodgrass has been assassinated, the Ick are leaderless and with no navy there is no empire. You saw what happened to our forces back there, if a hundred ships escaped, that's all." Captain Noble sighed. "The war is over and we lost."

"It's worse than that, both the Ick and the Federation Navies have been wiped out. Whoever controls those droids now controls the universe," Killashandra pointed out.

"Any word on Fo'c'sle survivors yet? Captain Noble asked.

"Kali and Cyborgpirate are confirmed lost, with the entire Fo'c'sle not here with us. We don't know about Grommit yet and the bounty hunter forces she was leading. We've had contact from half a dozen bounty hunters that managed to get clear," Killashandra said, putting her head in her hands. "We're done for. It's time to run and hide, as whoever controls that droid army is sure to send them looking for survivors."

General Jee sat in his office. He had managed to gather together a core of Federation ships and they had fought their way clear of the battle, their own droids' units swarming over them. Battles raged within their ships as droids tried to overthrow the human crews. The losses they had taken had been terrible and he now travelled with less than fifty battle cruisers, many of which were damaged and under-crewed. News was patchy as communication was badly interrupted, but they were picking up messages. Many planets across the Federation reported droid attacks, while there were rumours that the Federation Capital planet had been totally destroyed. There was a knock at the door and his security officer walked in and passed over a vid-screen.

"The information on the state of the ships we have with us; transferring crew to the least damaged ships, we will have thirty at full complement and another seven still at fighting capability, although we are without any fighter ships."

Jee shook his head. "How the hell did the Ick do this? And why betray their allies? It makes no sense."

"I don't believe it was the Ick, sir, we had probes out tracking the Ick fleet. Just before the droids turned on us, the Ick fleet changed course and speed. Our best intelligence from the final probe to pick them up reports them heading straight into an area of dead space," the security officer said nervously.

Jee sat back shocked, his mind reeling. "I want a new heading. Set course for the final confirmed co-ordinates of the Ick fleet. If this is true, then both the Federation and Ick have been destroyed, and there must be a third player. Have all the remaining assassins dispatched, we need information, and they are now our eyes and ears. We need to find out who is behind this as they are bound to continue the hunt for any survivors. Order the moving of crew, I just want space-worthy ships, as if we end up in another fight we can't look after any weak links. We set off to our new destination in thirty minutes, so get people moving. And see if you can make contact with the Ick command or any bounty hunters. We need a peace deal and to start working together, or at least pool what we do know."

"What of the people in the Inner Systems, General? We are getting reports of genocide by the droids," the security officer asked, avoiding looking at the general.

"Does it look like we can do anything?" General Jee said angrily. "We just got our ass handed to us on a plate by someone we didn't even know about. The planets will have to defend themselves the best they can."

# THE BIT AFTER THE END, THE WHAT'SIT.

The robot Kirk stood in front of the void. Behind him, behind the safety line, stood Frank and a number of other Ick scientists. It was Kirk's job to walk up to the void and then fire the bottle launcher into it, a daily job that filled him with a sense of importance. The truth was no one was sure of the effects of coming close to the void, so to save any future health problems, Kirk was the perfect choice. After shooting through the bottle Kirk stood and scanned the void, looking for any variations as instructed. Suddenly he picked up a change. Instead of nothingness he detected a series of chemicals in the void. Quickly he spun the top part of his body around and a small hatch on his chest opened from which he fired a small grappling hook that wrapped around a support strut for the void platform. Spinning his torso back around he dived forward and disappeared through the void.

Frank looked on in shock at the robot's actions, the other scientists equally baffled. The four marines stationed on the platform brought their weapons to bear and began to advance. Frank finally got over his shock and pushed a scientist out of the way to view the screen that was monitoring Kirk's scan. Quickly he came back to his own computer and began to type rapidly on the keyboard, ignoring the commotion that began around him as the Ick scientists began to question each other over what they had just seen the robot do. For some reason, when a science experiment didn't go to plan, all the scientists involved began to first cover their own backs and then work out a theory to sound as if they expected the unexpected turn in events.

Kirk fell through the void and then hit gravity again and landed on something soft. After a split second his robotic eye rebooted and he recognised the soft gasping object.

"Commander Alienbutt, it is you!" he said in his excited version of his monotone voice.

"Kirk," Alienbutt gasped, trying to get his breath back.

"You wouldn't believe what's been going on since we left you," Kirk said, rolling back off Alienbutt and landing on his feet.

"Later, cut the chains now before this whole place blows to Sung's anus," Alienbutt said desperately, looking at his wrist-com that now had the light blinking a fast red colour.

One of Kirk's fingers tips flipped back and a small laser cutter appeared. Kirk quickly cut through the chain holding Alienbutt's hand and then he began to toddle down to Alienbutt's feet.

"Did you hear Federal Entertainment One cancelled the Star Trek reruns? It's a good job I recorded them all, or the marines would be devastated. Those marines are such nice people; they love my film shows," Kirk said, cutting the chain at his feet. "We should be back in time for my showing of the new season of Star Trek Kirk's legacy. I know Kirk's played by an android, but..."

Alienbutt jumped down from the altar and quickly snatched the amulet from around Lucifus's neck and placed it back around his neck. Picking up Kirk he ran towards the void.

"Shut up and get us out of here. Rewind your cable now," he screamed as a loud rumbling began off in the distance and the inner sanctum of the temple began to shake. Kirk for once did as he was told without talking about it, and Alienbutt was pulled off his feet and dragged into the grey void as Kirk's line began to retract.

Frank watched as Kirk flew back through the void, a larger figure holding onto him. As they landed on the floor he hit the enter button on the keyboard. Seconds later a wall of white-hot flame burst through the void to hit the force field he had just erected. As he watched the screen before him he saw the shield begin to buckle, and transferred more power to it. Still the shields continued to buckle, but their rate had slowed. Transferring all but essential power into the shields, it finally stopped collapsing. The void platform was illuminated by the fireball and all averted their eyes, then the light disappeared and the platform was plunged into darkness. After a moment the transferred power returned and the lights came back on. Everyone on the platform stood blinking, trying to rid themselves of the afterglow of the fireball.

"Frank, please tell me you still have at least a dozen of those bottles of whiskey left, as Sung knows I need a drink," Alienbutt said, getting to his feet

Frank grinned before he replied. "I saved you some, and Kirk's had a pan of chilli sauce bubbling away for the last month. Welcome home, Alienbutt." Frank held up a bottle of whiskey. "I'm afraid we do have some real bad news."

Dream stood floating in space just beyond the void platform. Trobjorn floated beside him looking slightly worried.

"Will you stop worrying, this is your dream, Trobjorn, and nothing bad will happen to you," Dream said as they watched Alienbutt's return.

"It's not natural to float like this," Trobjorn said sullenly, looking down at the open space beneath his feet. He didn't know what vertigo was, and even someone who suffered from vertigo couldn't begin to understand what he thought when he looked down into the infinite drop. "And are you sure that creature can save your brother?" he asked, looking back to the events of Alienbutt's return.

"He's the only one that can return the Ick and revive their prophecy. Destiny should have known there was a second nexus. The prophecy reacted to it too late and didn't do enough to stop it. My brother and sister put too much of themselves into this duel prophecy idea, and its destruction by this feline Mr Fluffy has left him on the verge of extinction," Dream said, watching the events on the platform.

"Well they did drink a hell of a lot that night. So what do we do now?" Trobjorn asked.

"I'm going to give Fluffy a nice dream about bathing and bubble bath while you deliver my message," Dream replied. "He totally craps himself with that dream, and you should see the mess it makes when he has to clean himself up."
Trobjorn looked blankly at Dream, not really a cat type of person and knowing nothing of them.

"He has to lick himself clean," Dream said with an evil grin. "Now make sure you deliver my message when he goes to sleep and I'll be back to get you later." With that Dream disappeared, leaving Trobjorn alone

## Short Stories by Glenn

# Bleed with Style

Elohim is a rebellious teen. He does well in his studies, there was no disputing that, but he finds them far too easy and so he looks for other things to occupy his mind. Things like sneaking out and finding trouble – BIG trouble. His sister can't always be there to cover his back but she tries. One night he goes too far and the punishment is unexpected – life can be tough when you're a vampire.

### Available on Ebook in all formats.

# The Missing Sacrifice

A family holiday to Paris starts off well – until Eloim meets a sexy succubus on a boy's night out at an Abba tribute concert. Eloim's natural ability to find trouble reaches a new height as werewolves, demons and the greatest vampire hunters in Transylvania hunt for the cross dressing vampire teenager.

The second of the vampire Eloim short stories sees Eloim blunder through a plot to depose a king while struggling to stay as fashionable and stylish as only he can be.

Read more about Glenn and any future books on the Gingernut Books Website. Keep checking for news of Book three in the Alienbutt Saga.

**www.gingernutbooks.co.uk**

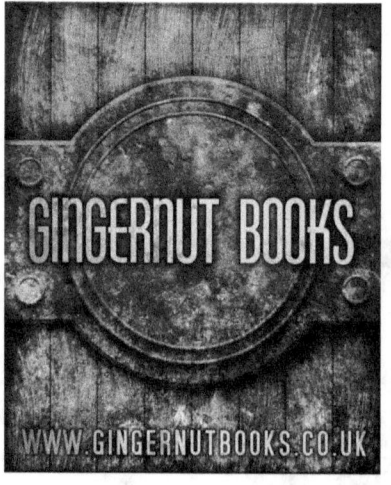

www.ingramcontent.com/pod-product-compliance
Lightning Source LLC
Chambersburg PA
CBHW060055150626
46556CB00017BA/735